Praise for FRIDAY BLACK

"If you like 'This Is America' [by Childish Gambino] you will love *Friday Black*."

Roxane Gay, author of *Hunger* and *Bad Feminist*

"Adjei-Brenyah has put readers on notice: his remarkable range, ingenious premises, and unflagging, momentous voice make this a first-rate collection."

Publishers' Weekly, starred review

"Prescient, dark, and deeply empathetic, visceral, and inventive, these stories announce Adjei-Brenyah as both an astute cultural critic and a truthteller."

Nafissa Thompson-Spires, author of *Heads of the Colored People*

"Adjei-Brenyah has a cool eye, bright mind, and high style. His stories are solid, they're unusual, imaginative, disturbing, wry, tender, funny. Bursting with surprising language and formal invention, they plant the zeitgeist onto the page. It lives in *Friday Black* in all its complexity, trouble and possibility. Writing this distinctive and good, especially in this uneasy time, is genuinely a cause for celebration."

Lynne Tillman, author of *Men and Apparitions*

FRIDAY BLACK

Nana Kwame Adjei-Brenyah

riverrun

First published in the USA in 2018 by
Houghton Mifflin Harcourt Publishing Company,
3 Park Avenue, 19th Floor, New York, New York 10016

First published in Great Britain in 2018 by

riverrun

An imprint of
Quercus Editions Limited
Carmelite House
50 Victoria Embankment
London EC4Y 0DZ

An Hachette UK company

A CIP catalogue record for this book is available
from the British Library

Hardback ISBN 978 1 78747 601 1
Ebook ISBN 978 1 78747 599 1

10 9 8 7 6 5 4 3 2 1

Printed and bound in Great Britain by Clays Ltd, Elcograf S.p.A.

For my mom, who said,
"How can you be bored?
How many books have you written?"

Anything you imagine, you possess

KENDRICK LAMAR

CONTENTS

FRIDAY BLACK

THE FINKELSTEIN 5

Fela, the headless girl, walked toward Emmanuel. Her neck jagged with red savagery. She was silent, but he could feel her waiting for him to do something, anything.

Then his phone rang, and he woke up.

He took a deep breath and set the Blackness in his voice down to a 1.5 on a 10-point scale. "Hi there, how are you doing today? Yes, yes, I did recently inquire about the status of my application. Well, all right, okay. Great to hear. I'll be there. Have a spectacular day." Emmanuel rolled out of bed and brushed his teeth. The house was quiet. His parents had already left for work.

That morning, like every morning, the first decision he made regarded his Blackness. His skin was a deep, constant brown. In public, when people could actually see him, it was impossible to get his Blackness down to anywhere near a 1.5. If he wore a tie, wing-tipped shoes, smiled constantly, used his indoor voice, and kept his hands strapped and calm at his sides, he could get his Blackness as low as 4.0.

Though Emmanuel was happy about scoring the interview, he also felt guilty about feeling happy about anything. Most

people he knew were still mourning the Finkelstein verdict: after twenty-eight minutes of deliberation, a jury of his peers
had acquitted George Wilson Dunn of any wrongdoing what-
soever. He had been indicted for allegedly using a chain saw to
hack off the heads of five black children outside the Finkelstein
Library in Valley Ridge, South Carolina. The court had ruled
that because the children were basically loitering and not actually inside the library reading, as one might expect of produc-
tive members of society, it was reasonable that Dunn had felt
threatened by these five black young people and, thus, he was
well within his rights when he protected himself, his library-
loaned DVDs, and his children by going into the back of his
Ford F-150 and retrieving his Hawtech PRO eighteen-inch 48cc
chain saw.

The case had seized the country by the ear and heart, and
was still, mostly, the only thing anyone was talking about. Finkelstein became the news cycle. On one side of the broadcast
world, anchors openly wept for the children, who were saints
in their eyes; on the opposite side were personalities like Brent
Kogan, the ever gruff and opinionated host of *What's the Big
Deal?*, who had said during an online panel discussion, "Yes,
yes, they were kids, but also, fuck niggers." Most news outlets
fell somewhere in between.

On verdict day, Emmanuel's family and friends of many
different races and backgrounds had gathered together and
watched a television tuned to a station that had sympathized
with the children, who were popularly known as the Finkelstein Five. Pizza and drinks were served. When the ruling was
announced, Emmanuel felt a clicking and grinding in his chest.
It burned. His mother, known to be one of the liveliest and
happiest women in the neighborhood, threw a plastic cup filled
with Coke across the room. When the plastic fell and the soda

splattered, the people stared at Emmanuel's mother. Seeing Mrs. Gyan that way meant it was real: they'd lost. Emmanuel's father walked away from the group wiping his eyes, and Emmanuel felt the grinding in his chest settle to a cold nothingness. On the ride home, his father cursed. His mother punched honks out of the steering wheel. Emmanuel breathed in and watched his hands appear, then disappear, then appear, then disappear as they rode past streetlights. He let the nothing he was feeling wash over him in one cold wave after another.

But now that he'd been called in for an interview with Stich's, a store self-described as an "innovator with a classic sensibility" that specialized in vintage sweaters, Emmanuel had something to think about besides the bodies of those kids, severed at the neck, growing damp in thick, pulsing, shooting blood. Instead, he thought about what to wear.

In a vague move of solidarity, Emmanuel climbed into the loose-fitting cargoes he'd worn on a camping trip. Then he stepped into his patent-leather Space Jams with the laces still clean and taut as they weaved up all across the black tongue. Next, he pulled out a long-ago abandoned black hoodie and dove into its tunnel. As a final act of solidarity, Emmanuel put on a gray snapback cap, a hat similar to the ones two of the Finkelstein Five had been wearing the day they were murdered —a fact George Wilson Dunn's defense had stressed throughout the proceedings.

Emmanuel stepped outside into the world, his Blackness at a solid 7.6. He felt like Evel Knievel at the top of a ramp. At the mall he'd look for something to wear to the interview, something to bring him down to at least a 4.2. He pulled the brim of his hat forward and down to shade his eyes. He walked up a hill toward Canfield Road, where he'd catch a bus. He listened to the gravel scraping under his sneakers. It had been a very long

time since he'd had his Blackness even close to a 7.0. "I want
you safe. You gotta know how to move," his father had said to
him at a very young age. Emmanuel started learning the basics
of his Blackness before he knew how to do long division: smiling when angry, whispering when he wanted to yell. Back when
he was in middle school, after a trip to the zoo, where he'd been
accused of stealing a stuffed panda from the gift shop, Emmanuel had burned his last pair of baggy jeans in his driveway. He'd
watched the denim curl and ash in front of him with unblinking eyes. When his father came outside, Emmanuel imagined
he'd get a good talking-to. Instead, his father stood quietly beside him. "This is an important thing to learn," his father had
said. Together they watched the fire until it ate itself dead.

It was crowded at the bus stop. He felt eyes shifting toward him
while pocketbooks shifted away. Emmanuel thought of George
Wilson Dunn. He imagined the middle-aged man standing
there in front of him, smiling, a chain saw growling in his
hands. He decided to try something dangerous: he turned his
hat backward so the shadow of the brim draped his neck. He
felt his Blackness leap and throb to an 8.0. The people grew
quiet. They tried to look superfriendly but also distant, as if he
were a tiger or an elephant they were watching beneath a big
tent. A path through the mass opened up for Emmanuel.
    Soon, he was standing near the bench. A young woman
with long brown hair and a guy wearing sunglasses above the
brim of his hat both remembered they had to be somewhere
else, immediately. An older woman remained sitting, and Emmanuel took the newly available seat beside her. The woman
glanced toward Emmanuel as he sat. She smiled faintly. Her
look of general disinterest made his heart sing. He turned his
hat forward and felt his Blackness ease back to a still very seri-

ous 7.6. A minute later, the brown-haired woman returned and sat beside him. She smiled like someone had told her that if she stopped smiling her frantic, wide-eyed smile Emmanuel would blow her brains out.

"The fact is, George Wilson Dunn is an American. Americans have the right to protect themselves," the defense attorney says in a singing, charming voice. "Do you have children? Do you have anyone you love? The prosecution has tried to beat you over the head with scary words like 'law' and 'murder' and 'sociopath.'" The defense attorney's index and middle fingers claw the air repeatedly to indicate quotations. "I'm here to tell you that this case isn't about any of those things. It's about an American man's right to love and protect his own life and the life of his beautiful baby girl and his handsome young son. So I ask you, what do you love more, the supposed 'law' or your children?"

"I object?," says the prosecuting attorney.

"I'll allow it, overruled," replies the judge as she dabs the now wet corners of her eyes. "Please continue, counselor."

"Thank you, Your Honor. I don't know about you all, but I love my children more than I love the 'law.' And I love America more than I love my children. That's what this case is about: love with a capital *L*. And America. That is what I'm defending here today. My client, Mister George Dunn, believed he was in danger. And you know what, if you believe something, anything, then that's what matters most. Believing. In America we have the freedom to believe. America, our beautiful sovereign state. Don't kill that here today."

The bus was pulling in. Emmanuel noticed a figure running toward the stop. It was Boogie, one of his best friends from back in grade school. In Ms. Fold's fourth-grade class, Emmanuel would peek over at Boogie's tests during their history exams and then angle his papers so Boogie could see his answers during math tests. In all the years he'd known Boogie, he'd never known him to dress in anything but too-large T-shirts and baggy sweats. By the time they were in high school, Emmanuel had learned to control his Blackness; Boogie had not. Emmanuel had quietly distanced himself from Boogie, who'd become known for fighting with other students and teachers. By now, he'd mostly forgotten about him, but when Emmanuel did think of Boogie, it was with pity for him and his static personhood. Boogie was always himself. Today, though, Boogie ran in black slacks, shining black dress shoes, a white button-up shirt, and a slim red tie. His dress combined with his sandy skin squeezed his Blackness down to a 2.9.

"Manny!" Boogie called as the bus pulled to a stop.

"What's good, bro," Emmanuel replied. In the past, Emmanuel had dialed his Blackness up whenever he was around Boogie. Today he didn't have to. People shuffled past them onto the bus. Emmanuel and Boogie clapped palms and held the grip so that, with their hands between them, their chests came together, and when they took their hands back, their fingers snapped against their palms.

Emmanuel said, "What you up to lately? What's new?"

"A lot, man. A lot. I've been waking up."

Emmanuel got on the bus, paid his $2.50, then found a seat near the back. Boogie took the empty seat beside him.

"Yeah?"

"Yeah, man. I've been working lately. I'm trying to get a lot of us together, man. We need to unify."

"Word," Emmanuel replied absently.

"I'm serious, bro. We need to move together. We got to now.

You've seen it. You know they don't give a fuck 'bout us now. They showed it." Emmanuel nodded. "We all need to unify. We need to wake the fuck up. I've been Naming. I'm getting a team together. You trying to ride or what?"

Emmanuel scanned the area around him to make sure no one had heard. It didn't seem like anyone had, but still he regretted his proximity to Boogie. "You're not really doing that Naming stuff?" Emmanuel watched the smile on Boogie's face melt. Emmanuel made sure his face didn't do anything at all.

"Of course I am." Boogie unbuttoned the left cuff of his shirt and pulled the sleeve up. Along Boogie's inner forearm were three different marks. Each of them was a very distinct 5 carved and scarred into his skin. After it was clear Emmanuel had seen, Boogie smoothed his sleeve back down over his arm but did not button the cuff. He continued in a low voice. "You know what my uncle said to me the other day?"

Emmanuel waited.

"He said that when you're on the bus and a tired man is kinda leaning over beside you, using your shoulder like a pillow, people tell you to wake him up. They'll try to sell it to you that the man needs to wake up and find some other place to rest 'cause you ain't a goddamn mattress."

Emmanuel made a sound to show he was following.

"But if he's sleeping on his own, not bothering you, it's supposed to be different. And if that sleeping man gets ran up on by somebody that wants to take advantage of him 'cause he's asleep, 'cause he's so tired, everybody tries to tell you we're supposed to be, like, 'That's not my problem, that don't got a thing to do with me,' as he gets his pockets all the way ran through or worse.

"That man sleeping on the bus, he's your brother. That's what my uncle's saying. You need to protect him. Yeah, you

might need to wake him up, but while he's asleep, he's your re-
sponsibility. Your brother, even if you ain't met him a day in
your life, is your business. Feel me?"

Emmanuel made another confirmatory sound.

Two days after the ruling, the first report had come through.
An elderly white couple, both in their sixties, had had their
brains smashed in by a group armed with bricks and rusty
metal pipes. Witnesses said the murderers had been dressed in
very fancy clothes: bow ties and summer hats, cuff links and
high heels. Throughout the double murder, the group/gang had
chanted, "Mboya! Mboya! Tyler Kenneth Mboya," the name of
the eldest boy killed at Finkelstein. The next day a similar story
broke. Three white schoolgirls had been killed with ice picks.
A black man and black woman had poked holes through the
girls' skulls like they were mining for diamonds. They chanted
"Akua Harris, Akua Harris, Akua Harris" all through the murder, according to reports. Again, the killers had been described
as "quite fashionable, given the circumstances." In both cases,
the killers had been caught immediately following the act. The
couple that killed the schoolgirls had carved the number 5 into
their own skins just before the attack.

Several more cases of beatings and killings followed the first
two. Each time the culprits screamed the name of one of the
Finkelstein Five. The Namers became the latest terrorists on
the news. Most of the perpetrators were killed by police officers before they could be brought in for questioning. Those
who were detained spoke only the name of the child they'd
used as a mantra to their violence. None seemed interested in
defense.

By far, the most famous of the Namers was Mary "Mistress" Redding. The story was, Mistress Redding had been de-

tained wearing a single bloodstained white silk glove over her left hand, once-sparkling white shoes with four-inch heels, and an A-line dress that was such a hard, rusty red that officers couldn't believe it had originally been a perfect white. For hours, Redding answered all of the questions with a single name. *Why did you do it?* "J. D. Heroy." *He was just a child! How could you?* "J. D. Heroy." *Who are you working with? Who is your leader?* "J. D. Heroy." *Do you feel any remorse for what you've done?* "J. D. Heroy." *What is it you people want?* "J. D. Heroy." Redding had been caught with a group that had killed a single teenage boy, but there was a train of ten 5s carved into her back that trailed down to her left thigh, including one that was dripping and fresh when she was caught. According to reports, several hours into an advanced interrogation session, a single sentence had escaped Mistress Redding. "If I had words left in me, I would not be here."

Emmanuel remembered how the news had reported the bloody phenomenon: "Breaking this evening," said one anchor, "yet another innocent child was mercilessly beaten by a gang of thugs, all of whom seem, again, to be descendants of the African diaspora. What do you think of this, Holly?"

"Well, many people in the streets are saying, and I quote, 'I told you they don't know how to act! We told you.' Beyond that, all I can say is this violence is terrible." The coanchor shook her head, disgusted.

The names of each of the Finkelstein Five had become curses. When no one was around, Emmanuel liked to say the names to himself: Tyler Mboya, Fela St. John, Akua Harris, Marcus Harris, J. D. Heroy.

"This is just the beginning," Boogie said. He pulled a small box cutter out of his pocket. Emmanuel almost made a sound, but Boogie said, "Don't worry, I'm not gonna use it. Not here. I haven't gone all the way — yet." Emmanuel watched Boogie as he rolled up his sleeve for the second time and, with a practiced precision, used five quick slashes to cut a small 5 into his left arm. The skin split into a thin red that gathered, then rolled down the side of his arm.

Boogie reached over Emmanuel and pulled the yellow cord. There was a *bing* sound and the STOP REQUESTED sign went bright. The bus slowed in front of Market Plaza.

"I'm gonna hit you up later, Manny. We're going to need you."

"Got it. I have the same number," Emmanuel said as the bus stopped.

Boogie walked to the bus's rear door. He turned, smiled at Emmanuel, then at the top of his lungs screamed, "J. D. HE-ROY!" The name was still echoing off the windows when Boogie took his fist and crashed it against a white woman's jaw. She didn't make a sound. She slumped over in her seat. Boogie pulled his fist back again and punched the woman in the face a second time. A third. It sounded like hammering a nail into soft wood.

"Help!" somebody sitting near the woman screamed. "Fuck you, asshole," another yelled as Boogie jumped out the bus's back door and sprinted away. No one followed him. Emmanuel pulled his cell phone out of his pocket and dialed 911. As he called, he stepped toward the crowd that had formed around the woman. Her nose was busted and bleeding. The blood rolled out in a steady leak and had bubbles in it. Again, Emmanuel felt a ticking and grinding in his chest. He gritted his teeth and closed his eyes. He imagined the color sky blue.

"Hi. I'm on a bus and this lady is hurt. Yeah, we're on Myrtle, right by Market Plaza. Yeah, she's hurt pretty bad." He could feel fear swelling toward him. He'd been next to Boogie and at 7.6. The bus sat on the roadside, and a small group of passengers made a wall around the woman. The other passengers took turns shooting hard stares at Emmanuel. He imagined the police officers blasting through the bus doors and the many fingers that would immediately point in his direction. He imagined the bullet that would not take even a second to find his brain. He'd never stolen a thing in his life; he didn't even particularly like pandas. He got off the bus, ignoring the murmurs and trying hard not to look at the woman with the broken face. He walked a few blocks to a nearby bus stop.

The mall was as it always was. Parents ran from store to store; their children struggled to keep pace. Three security guards tailed Emmanuel from the moment he stepped into the mall. Whenever he slowed or stopped, the guards jumped into conversation or pretended to listen to important information via their two-way radios. Normally, when Emmanuel went to the mall, he wore blue jeans that weren't too baggy or tight and a nice collared shirt. He smiled ear to ear and walked very slowly, only eyeing any one thing in any store for a maximum of twelve seconds. Emmanuel's usual mall Blackness was a smooth 5.0. Usually only one security guard followed him.

He went into a store named Rodger's. He chose an eggshell blue button-up, then handed the shirt to a cashier. The cashier took his card and ran it through the machine. Then she folded his shirt and tucked it into a plastic bag.

"I need a receipt," Emmanuel said, then thanked her as she handed him the flimsy white paper. He dropped it into the bag with his shirt. When he approached the store's entrance/exit, he felt a tug on his wrist. He turned to see a tall man with a store name tag pinned to his shirt.

"Did you purchase that shirt, sir?" The man's voice was condescending and sharp, like a cruel teacher's or a villain's from a children's television show. Immediately, Emmanuel felt habit telling him to be precisely gentle, to smile, and not to yell no matter what. He pushed habit away as he snatched his hand back from the man.

"Yeah, actually I did," Emmanuel said in a voice loud enough to make shoppers turn and stare.

"Do you have a receipt for that purchase that you actually made?"

"Yes, I do."

"Can I please see this receipt that you actually have for that purchase you actually made?"

"Well, I can show it to you," Emmanuel began. "Or maybe ask the cashier who rang me up two seconds ago." He jabbed a finger in the direction of the register. He felt his Blackness creeping up toward 8.1. He was angry and alive and free. When the cashier looked up and saw what was happening, she raised a hand and waved with her fingers.

"Hmm, so do you have a receipt or not?"

Emmanuel stared at the man. Then he handed him the receipt. Emmanuel had had this conversation a number of times before. Not so much since he'd really learned to lock down to sub-6.0 levels.

"Can't be too careful," the man said, and handed the receipt back. Emmanuel knew better than to wait for an apology. He turned and left the store and felt himself slide back down to a 7.6 in the eyes of the mallgoers around him.

As Emmanuel made his way back to the bus stop, a different pair of security guards followed closely behind him, but far enough away to make it seem like they were just walking in the same direction he was. Emmanuel stopped to tie his shoe, and one of the security guards jumped behind a decorative potted plant while the other stared off into the sky, whistling. They followed him to the south exit bus stop, then turned back into the mall once he was seated beneath the overhang.

Emmanuel found a window seat. No one sat next to him. The bus had just started moving when his phone buzzed. He recognized the number as the same one that had called him that morning. He pushed the green dot on the screen, immediately setting his voice to a 1.5.

"Hello. You've reached Emmanuel."

"Hey there, son, I called this morning about an interview we thought about lining up for you." The man's voice was full and husky.

"Yes, I'm looking forward to it. Tomorrow at eleven, correct?"

"Well, the thing is and—I really hate to be this guy, but I just thought I might save you some time. It's Emmanuel Gyan, right?"

"Yes, that's correct."

"Well, Emmanuel, thing is, and shit, I didn't think things all the way through, but I think we might have that position filled already."

"Pardon?"

"Well, thing is, we have this guy Jamaal here already, and then there's also Ty, who's half-Egyptian. So I mean, it'd be overkill. We aren't an urban brand. You know what I mean? So I thought it'd—" Emmanuel ended the call and tried very hard to breathe. Again, his phone buzzed. He eyed the screen hard; it was a message from Boogie. *The park 10:45.*

———

"Mister Dunn." The defense attorney sashays to the bench.
"What were you doing on the night in question before you en-
countered the five people you say attacked you?"

"Well." George Wilson Dunn looks at his attorney, then at
the jury. "I was with my children at the library. Both of them.
Tiffany and Rodman. I'm a single father."

"A single father out with his children at the library. So what
happened before you went outside?" The defense attorney
looks curious, as if this were all news to him.

"Thing is, being a father is the most important thing in the
world to me. And being a father of two kids like Tiffany and
Rodman, you just never know what you're going to get.

"That night, as we're looking around the movie section for
something to watch that weekend, Tiffany out and says she's
not going to school anymore 'cause she's fat and ugly, and all
of a sudden I've got this crisis on my hands. And she's the older
one, usually gives me less trouble. But that's being a parent. No
prep. She's never said anything like this before, and all of a sudden you have to fix it or else she'll become some kinda bum or
crack whore."

"This is irrelevant, Your Honor," the prosecuting attorney
says from her chair.

"I'll allow it, but get on with your story, Mister Dunn."

"This *is* the story," Dunn says. "So outta nowhere I gotta figure out something to say to my only daughter to put her back
on track. And all the while, my only boy, he's quiet and not
saying a word this whole time, and that has me almost more
worried than anything else. I love the kid, but he's a crazy one.
So as we're getting ready to leave the library, I tell Tiffany how
she's beautiful and how Daddy loves her and how that will
never change. And you know what she says? She says, 'Okay,'
like it's all fixed. Like she just wanted me to say that one thing.

And I can finally breathe. Then the other one, Rodman, pushes over a cart that crashes into a shelf and makes about a hundred DVDs crash down to the floor. But that's being a parent, ya know? Anyway, that's what happened before I got outside."

"All right, and when you were outside?" the defense asks with a warm smile.

"When I got outside, I was attacked. And I protected myself and both my kids."

"And, on this night in question, were your actions motivated by the love you feel for your children and your God-given right to protect yourself and them?"

"They were."

"No further questions, Mister Dunn."

Emmanuel greeted his parents with a smile when they got home. They ate dinner together as a family, though Emmanuel hardly spoke a word. After they were finished, Emmanuel's father told him he was proud of him no matter what happened at the interview and that he should wear a tie and try to speak slowly. "You'll do great," he said.

When his parents were asleep, Emmanuel slipped into the shower. He got out, combed his hair, then put on fresh underwear and socks. He pulled and zipped himself into ironed tan slacks. He looped a brown leather belt around his waist. Then he put on a white undershirt and the eggshell blue button-up. He tied the laces of his wing-tipped dress shoes tightly.

Emmanuel moved slowly out of his room and out of the house. He closed the side door as quietly as he could manage and was in the garage. There was an aluminum bat leaning against a wall with peeling paint. He stared at the bat. The grinding, clicking heat in his chest hadn't stopped churning since he'd gotten off the bus. It made him feel like the bat would cure everything if he could just grab it and bring it with him to the park. Emmanuel walked toward the bat, then thought better of it. He left his home empty-handed and headed toward Marshall Park.

"Mister Dunn, please recount the night of July the thirteenth."

George Dunn sits on the stand looking sweaty and apologetic. Apologetic in an I-sure-am-sorry-acting-well-within-my-rights-caused-all-this-gosh-darn-hoopla kind of way.

"Well, I was with my two kids—Tiffany and Rodman—when I saw a gang laughing and doing God knows what outside the library."

"Did you at any point feel threatened, Mister Dunn?"

"Well, I didn't at first, but then I realized all five of them were wearing black, like they were about to commit a robbery."

"Are you suggesting that it was these young people's clothes that made them a threat to you and your family?" The prosecution has been waiting for this moment for weeks.

"No, no. Of course not. It was when one of them, the tall one, started yelling stuff at me. I was afraid for my children—Tiffany and Rodman. That's all I was thinking: Tiffany, Rodman. I had to protect them." Several members of the jury nod thoughtfully.

"And what did Mister Heroy yell at you?"

"I think he wanted my money—or my car. He said, 'Gimme,' and then something else."

"So at what point did you feel your life was threatened?"

"I wasn't about to wait until I saw my life flashing before my eyes. Or Tiffany's or Rodman's. I had to act. I did what I did for them."

"And what did you do?"

"I went and got my saw." Dunn's eyes glow. "I did what I had to do. And you know what—I loved protecting my kids."

The jury stares, attentive, almost breathless. Engaged and excited.

The night was cool. Under an unspectacular sky, Emmanuel felt the story of the Finkelstein Five on his fingers and in his chest and in each of his breaths. He imagined George Wilson Dunn walking free down the courtroom steps as cameras flashed. Emmanuel turned around and went back to his garage where the bat was waiting for him. It was from his Little League days. He'd played second base. The bat was too big for him then, too heavy. Now it was just right. He took it and walked to the park. I'm awake now; Boogie had said something like that while they were on the bus.

"Looking like a young Hank Aaron, bro," Boogie said as Emmanuel approached. With Boogie was a middle school biology teacher Emmanuel remembered as Mr. Coder, as well as a girl named Tisha, Boogie's girlfriend, and another tiny man with glasses. Mr. Coder and the tiny man each wore three-piece suits, navy blue and coal black respectively. Their eyes looked cold and dead. Tisha wore a flowing yellow dress with a festive hat that had a kind of veil that swooped across the front of it. On her left hand was an elegant white glove. Boogie was wearing the same white shirt and slim red tie he'd had on that morning. *Gang.* That was the word they'd use.

"My bro Manny has the right idea," Boogie said after a quick exchanging of names. "Today we're going all the way. I hope you know how to swing that thing." Boogie crouched into a stance and rocked an imaginary bat back and forth like Ken Griffey Jr. Then he took a hard step into an invisible fastball that he crushed into the cheap seats. Emmanuel's body tensed. Boogie laughed and ran around a tiny diamond. "All the way," he said as he rounded the bases.

"So you've grabbed your chain saw. What happens next?"

"The tall one, he was so tall, he must have been a basketball player or something, he says he's not scared of no hedge cutter, and he comes charging at me."

"So an unarmed J. D. Heroy came charging at you while you were holding a chain saw—totally unprovoked."

"Totally."

"What happened next?"

"*Vroom*, I had my young children, Tiffany and Rodman, behind me so I could, *vroom, vroom,* protect them."

"What exactly does that mean?"

"That I revved my saw and got to cutting."

"You 'got to cutting'? Please, Mister Dunn. Please be specific."

"*Vroom*. I cut that basketball player's head clean, *vroom,* off."

"And then what?"

"Then three more of them rushed me. They tried to jump me."

"And as these children were running toward you, what did you do? Did you ever think to run? Get into your truck and go?"

"Well, I checked to see if Tiffany and Rodman were safe, and then I went to make sure they stayed safe. I was too worried about my kids to think about running."

"And how did you 'make sure they stayed safe,' Mister Dunn?"

"I got to cutting." George Dunn pantomimes pulling the rip cord of a chain saw several times.

"You mutilated five children."

"I protected my children."

Emmanuel was surprised to see he was the only one of the group who carried a weapon. He felt a strange pride.

"So where are we getting them?" Mr. Coder asked.

"Right here. We'll wait in Tisha's car for a couple to come round trying to use their car as a love box. This is the spot for that," Boogie said. He pinched Tisha's side.

"I want to know who we're Naming," Tisha said, swatting Boogie's hand away playfully. "That matters," she finished, her voice dropping to seriousness.

"And what about Fela St. John?" the prosecution asks, finally.

"Which one is that?" George Dunn replies quickly.

The prosecuting attorney smiles, her eyes are bright and unflinching. "The seven-year-old girl. The cousin of Akua and Marcus Harris. What about the seven-year-old girl you decapitated with a chain saw?"

"She looked a lot older than seven to me," Dunn replies.

"Of course. How old did you think she was as you pulled the blade through her neck?"

"Maybe thirteen or even fourteen."

"Maybe thirteen or fourteen. And you approached her—you ran after her and murdered her. The reports show you killed her last and that she was found yards from the rest. Did you have to chase her? How fast was she?"

"She didn't run anywhere. Tried to attack me, same as the rest of them."

"Fela St. John, the seven-year-old girl, tried to attack you, a grown man who she had just watched murder some of her friends and family. And somehow her body was found in a completely different area. Do you think that adds up? Does that sound like a seven-year-old girl to you?"

"She looked at least thirteen."

"Does that sound like a thirteen-year-old girl to you, Mister Dunn?"

"These days," Dunn says, "you just never know."

"Fela," Emmanuel said. "Fela St. John." He could see those news photos of her in her Sunday best: a shining yellow dress and bright barrettes in her hair. Then the pictures that had leaked to the internet: her tiny frame dressed in blood, headless.

"Okay. Now we just gotta wait," Boogie said. He started walking toward Tisha's car. The group followed. "When they get going, we're gonna run up on them, crack open a window, and pull 'em out. No playing around. We're doing this right."

They didn't have to wait very long. The couple looked young. Emmanuel only glimpsed them for a second as they turned hard into the parking lot. They parked, and soon their silver sedan was bouncing gently. All Emmanuel knew for sure was that one had brown hair and the other blonde.

"All right, I want to put it in blood real quick," said Boogie as he pulled a small box cutter from the glove compartment. He handed the cutter to Tisha, who took his right forearm. She brought the blade to his skin and, with surprising ease, cut a large 5 into him. "It feels good, I swear," Boogie said as he bit his lip and looked into the rearview. Once Tisha was finished, she handed the cutter to Boogie, who scooted closer to her and reached over the middle console so he could carve a 5 into Tisha's shoulder. "It's gonna be okay; don't be nervous," Boogie said. Tisha took several sharp breaths in, then exhaled in a great wave once he was finished. Emmanuel could see the 5 sprout up in red. Boogie turned in his seat to hand Mr. Coder the blade. "Shit, they look like they might be getting ready to dip, we gotta move." Boogie took his blade back, then looked at Emmanuel. "Hit those windows," Boogie said to Emmanuel, who was sandwiched between the two older men. "Then we'll pull 'em out."

Boogie unlocked and opened his door first, then Tisha opened hers. The air that flooded into the car felt charged. Emmanuel waited for the two men sitting on either side of him to open their doors. The group of them walked slowly across the lot. The bopping stopped. They knew. *Fela St. John.* He said the name to clear his head. *Fela St. John. Fela St. John.* Emmanuel imagined the fear the couple in the car might be feeling. He imagined each of the Finkelstein Five. Emmanuel ran forward and, with a force he imagined could crush anything, swung his bat into the rear window on the right side. The bat met the glass and clanked. His body was tingling with energy, and where there had been grinding and heat, there was an explosion. "Fela St. John!" he roared, and swung at the window a second time. It shattered, and suddenly the night was aflame with screams.

"Oh shit!" a voice from the car screamed. The other screamed in the language of fear. No words.

"Fela St. John," Emmanuel screamed from somewhere deep inside himself. He ran to the other side of the car and smashed the other rear window in three swings. The screams, already impossibly loud, doubled in intensity. Everything sounded like everything else. The other door was open, then closed, open, then closed, in a tug of war between Boogie and the man in the car.

"FELA ST. JOHN!" Boogie yelled, pulling the man's torso and head out of the car. His arm still gripped the door. Boogie raised his foot and kicked hard at the top of his head. Tisha did the same; she wore wedges that fell on the man's head like bricks. Red blood drizzled the concrete. After a few more stomps, he seemed mostly powerless and let them drag his body out. The man in the glasses and Mr. Coder had the other door open and pulled out the woman, a young girl, maybe in college, who was kicking and yelling sounds that Emmanuel had heard only in horror movies.

"I beg of you, I implore you, not to consider anything but the facts," the prosecutor says to begin her closing. "Over the last several days, we've heard the accused try to wiggle out of one simple fact: he murdered five children completely unprovoked. He may think his chain saw some holy weapon or a scepter bestowed on him by God, but don't let him go on believing that. Please don't let the blood of these five children—with all the potential in the world—spill into nothingness. Please show us that they mattered. These children who were killed before they ever got a chance to know the world, to love, to hate, to laugh, to cry, to see all the things that we've seen, and finally decide what kinds of people they might want to be. They mattered. Don't let their deaths go unpunished.

"We have a system that, though it can never ease the pain, tries to right the wrongs. We have a system that, though it won't ever succeed, attempts valiantly to fill this all-consuming void torn into the heart of the world by men like George Wilson Dunn. I happen to be one of the people who are perhaps foolish enough to believe there is a difference between good and evil. Somehow. Still. Please show me I'm not a fool. Show the parents of these children they aren't fools for demanding justice. For knowing the idea of justice was born for them and this very moment. Mister George Dunn destroyed something. Maybe the only sacred thing. Show him it matters. Show him that you know these children, Tyler Mboya, Fela St. John, Akua Harris, Marcus Harris, and J. D. Heroy were humans with a heart, just like any one of you."

The two white bodies huddled together, trapped in a circle of Emmanuel and the rest of them. The man was crying. His face was bruised. Red flowed from his nose to his lips. He'd been bargaining for the last minute.

"Please, please! What can we give you?" His body shook. "Please, it's yours. Please!" The woman huddled on the ground beside him made raspy, choking sounds.

"Fela, Fela, Fela." It was a trance. Emmanuel tried to look at the eyes of the young couple. He smashed his bat against the concrete several times while yelling the name. The bat bouncing off the ground sang a metallic yelp and shocked electricity into his veins.

"Say it for me," Emmanuel said suddenly. A screeching, crazy voice came from a part of him he was just discovering, but which he understood had been growing for a very long time. "Say her name," Emmanuel said. He pointed his bat at the couple. "Say her name for me. I need to hear it." He raised his bat, and both the white bodies flinched in response. He crashed the bat down. He felt the bark of the bat against the concrete. *This is what it is to be the wolf,* the bat screamed. *You have been the sheep, but now you are the wolf.* "SAY IT FOR ME. I BEG OF YOU," Emmanuel screamed. This, he knew, was going all the way. He could feel the group feed on his fury. "Fela St. John, Fela St. John, Fela St. John," they chanted in praise. "Tell me you love her," Emmanuel said. "Tell me I'm crazy. I'm begging you. Say her name." Emmanuel looked down at the tears and the red that seemed to be all that was left of the couple. They weren't even people. Just pumping hearts, hormones. He wondered if his rage would end; he imagined it leaking out of him.

He figured that at the other side of the tunnel—after the Naming—he might be happy. But as he thrashed and yelled and saw it all, he felt nothing leaving him. There was only throbbing. Yelling and screaming and banging a bat on the ground, he thought that maybe he was being exactly who he really was for once. Doing exactly what was expected of him. The screaming of the couple there, the honesty of their fear— he felt it giving him wings.

Boogie, standing beside Emmanuel, motioned for him to hand the bat over so he could finish what they'd started. Emmanuel looked toward the weeping man. His shirt was on backward. The woman was quieting down. She did not have much more breath to give. But in the middle of all those sounds of rage, timidly but definitely, Emmanuel heard something come from the woman's mouth.

"Fela St. John," the woman said. And as she did, Emmanuel looked into the eyes of the woman, and she looked back into his.

"Let me get that," Boogie screamed, opening his palms to receive the bat. "I want to be the one. I want to feel it. Please let me. Please." When Emmanuel did not hand the bat over, Boogie's fire blazed brighter. "This can't wait. I need this now," he said as he pulled out the box cutter. "I'll start it," Boogie said, looking at Emmanuel.

Emmanuel gripped the bat. Boogie's eyes were large and

heavy as he turned toward the couple. The blade in his fist grew as his thumb pushed at the box cutter. He stepped forward.

"I don't know what to do!" Emmanuel screamed, and swung the bat full force, cutting the wind in half and hitting Boogie in the flank, crashing the bat at his ribs. The box cutter fell to the floor.

"Ladies and gentlemen. Gentlemen and ladies." The defense stands, strides toward the jurors, adjusts the knot of his tie then continues, "The prosecution has tried to prove that George Dunn is a monster incapable of love. A monster that would hack down five helpless children. But what the prosecution has failed to do is prove that he was not a hero saving his children from five monsters. That may sound harsh, but let's be honest. We've seen this story before. A hardworking middle-class white man is put in a situation where he has to defend himself. And all of a sudden he's a 'racist.' All of a sudden he's a 'murderer.' No motive, no prior history, except for several ridiculous stories concocted by so-called 'childhood friends' and so-called 'family members.' It's all very convenient, I think. That all these facts and testimonies suddenly align perfectly to incriminate a man who was spending an evening with his children. Before you make your decision, I want you to remember a single word: freedom. It sounds better than prison or death or fear, doesn't it? Freedom just has a certain ring to it, doesn't it? Bring freedom. Please, please freedom."

Boogie fell to the ground in a heap. "Goddamn it," he screamed. Breathing seemed to be hard for him. Tisha yelled, then crawled to Boogie's side on the ground. Her yellow dress puddled around her. Boogie mumbled violent words as he writhed in the middle of a small sun in Tisha's arms. Mr. Coder and the man in glasses stood without moving. The white couple was now completely silent.

Emmanuel took two steps, dragging the bat on the ground. He stood above the couple. "Fela St. John, Fela St. John!" the couple screamed. Emmanuel looked down on them and saw himself in their eyes. He was the wolf. He felt the bat in his hands. He wanted to stand there forever. He wanted to scream and feel all their fear in his stomach till he burst.

Emmanuel looked around. He heard the screams of police vehicles more clearly now. Mr. Coder and the other man were running away. He heard the sirens, and for the first time in his life, Emmanuel did not fear them.

"Put your hands in the air," a giant voice, one from an entirely different world, said. Emmanuel smiled. He very slowly raised both of his arms. Tisha cried quietly over Boogie, who was still mumbling in a dream.

"Drop the weapon," the voice called. Red and blue lights tie-dyed it all.

"Fela St.—" Emmanuel began as he dropped the bat with his hands held above his head. He thought of the names. Then he felt it. The feeling of his Blackness rising to an almighty 10.0. He heard a boom that was like the child of thunder. He saw his own brain burst ahead of him. Hardy red confetti. His blood splashed all over the pavement and the couple. He saw the Finkelstein Five dancing around him: Tyler Mboya, Akua Harris, J. D. Heroy, Marcus Harris, Fela St. John. They told him they loved him, still, forever. In that moment, with his final thoughts, his last feelings as a member of the world, Emmanuel felt his Blackness slide and plummet to an absolute nothing point nothing.

THINGS MY MOTHER SAID

My mother's favorite thing to say to me was "I am not your friend." She'd often say, "You are my firstborn son, my only son," as a reminder not to die. She loved saying, as a way to keep me humble, "I didn't have a mother. You're lucky. You have a mother."

When the TV went dark, my mother said, "Good. Now you can read more." Then our house at the bottom of a hill lost all its life: gas, water, electric.

One day I came home to the warm smell of chicken and rice. I hadn't been able to steal a second burger in the cafeteria at school that day. My stomach whined. At home the fridge had become a casket bearing nothing. The range and oven had become decorations meant to make a dying box look like a home. Hunger colored those days.

"Where is this from?" I asked, already carving out a healthy portion from a worn gray pot.

My mother pretended she didn't hear me. She was studying the pages of her massive white Bible at the kitchen table. Wide sheets of light pressed through the window and draped her. She spent her days reading that big Bible. Its pages wore to film as her fingers fluttered from psalm to psalm. She'd be asleep by the splash of dusk. I, on the other hand, would be up for hours. Trying to do homework by the blue glow of my cell phone, clinging to its light until it died. At night hunger and I huddled together. I'd fall asleep thinking one day I would change everything.

That afternoon I ate the chicken and rice. It tasted like pepper and smoke. "How did you make this, Mom?" I asked again. She looked up from her Bible. "*Auwrade*. Did you pray over your food? Did you say your psalms today?" I ate the food quickly, greedily. I chewed the bones till they splintered in my mouth.

Another thing my mother often said: "You are the best thing that ever happened to me."

Later, when I was in the backyard, hesitant to return to the dying box as the sun dipped away, I found a patch of charred grass and a small circle of blackened stones and pebbles. An ash moon branded into a sea of wild green grass. I touched a gray rock partially blackened by flame to see if it was still hot. I felt proud and ashamed.

For the record, I know I was lucky, I know I am lucky, I don't think you're stupid, I know I am not your friend, I hope you can be proud of me.

THE ERA

S uck one and die," says Scotty, a tall, mostly true, kid. "I'm aggressive 'cause I think you don't know shit."
       We're in HowItWas class.
    "Well," Mr. Harper says, twisting his ugly body toward us. "You should shut your mouth because you're a youth-teen who doesn't know shit about shit and I'm a full-middler who's been teaching this stuff for more years than I'm proud of."
    "Understood," says Scotty.
    Then Mr. Harper went back to talking about the time before the Turn, which came after the Big Quick War, which came after the Long Big War. I was thinking about going to the nurse for some prelunch Good. I do bad at school because sometimes I think when I should be learning.
    "So after the Big Quick," Mr. Harper continues in his bored voice, "science and philosopher guys realized that people had been living wrong the whole time before. Sacrificing themselves, their efficiency, and their wants. This made a world of distrust and misfortune, which led to the Big Wars.
    "Back then, everyone was a liar. It was so bad that it would not have been uncommon for people to tell Samantha"—Mr.

Harper points a finger at Samantha, who sits next to me—
"that she was beautiful even though, obviously, she is hideous."
Samantha nods her ugly head to show she understands. Her
face is squished so bad she's always looking in two different directions. Sometimes, kids who get prebirth optiselected come
out all messed up. Samantha is "unoptimal." That's the official
name for people like her, whose optimization screwed up and
made their bodies horrible. I don't have any gene corrections. I
wasn't optimized at all. I am not optimal or ideal. But I'm also
not unoptimal, so I wasn't going to look like Samantha, which
is good. It's not all good, though, since no optiselect means no
chance of being perfect either. I don't care. I'm true. I'm proud,
still. Looking over, being nosy 'cause sometimes I do that, I
see Samantha log into her class pad: *I would have been pretty/
beautiful.*

   "Or"—and now Mr. Harper is looking at me; I can feel him
thinking me into an example—"back then a teacher might've
told Ben, who we know is a dummy, that he was smart or that
if he would just apply himself he'd do better." The class laughs
'cause they think a world where I'm smart is hee-haw. In my
head I think, *Mr. Harper, do you think that back then students
would think you were something other than a fat, ugly skin
sack?* Then I say, "Mr. Harper, do you think back then students would think you were something other than a fat, ugly
skin sack?"

   "I don't know what they'd say about me," Mr. Harper says.
"Probably that it was a great thing that I was a teacher and that
my life wasn't trash. Anything else, Ben?" I start to say something else about how they must have really, really liked lying
to say Mr. Harper was a good teacher, but I don't say that out
loud because, even though I'm being true, they'd say I was being emotional and it was clouding my truth.

"I understand," I say.

Being emotional isn't prideful, and being truthful, prideful, and intelligent are the best things. I'm truthful and prideful as best as I can be. Emotional truth-clouding was the main thing that led to the Long Big War and the Big Quick War.

They're called the Water Wars because of how the Old Federation lied to its own people about how the Amalgamation of Allies had poisoned the water reservoirs. The result was catastrophic/horrific. Then, since the people of the Old Federation were mad because of their own truth-clouding, they kept on warring for years and years, and the Old Federation became the New Federation that stands proudly today. Later on, when the Amalgamation of Allies suspected a key reservoir had been poisoned, they asked the New Federation if they'd done it. In a stunning act of graciousness and honesty, my New Federation ancestors told the truth, said, "Yeah, we did poison that reservoir," and, in doing so, saved many, many lives that were later more honorably destroyed via nuclear. The wars going on now, Valid Storm Alpha and the True Freedom Campaign, are valid/true wars because we know we aren't being emotional fighting them.

"Class, please scroll to chapter forty-one and take it in," Mr. Harper says. The class touches their note-screens. The chapter is thirty-eight pages. I don't even try to read it. I look at some chapter videos of people doing things they used to do: a man throws three balls into the air, a woman in a dress spins on one leg. After three minutes, the class is done reading the chapter. Their SpeedRead™ chips make reading easy/quick for them. SpeedRead™ lets optimized people take in words faster than I can hardly see them. Since I'm a clear-born, I look while they read. I will read the chapters on my own later. But even staring at the videos and pictures is better than some can do. Saman-

tha can't hardly look at her screen. And then there's Nick and
Raphy, who are the class shoelookers. All they do is cry and
moan. They were both optimized and still became shoelookers.
Being emotional is all they are, and it means they aren't good
for anything. I'm glad Samantha and Nick and Raphy are in
the class. Because of them, I'm not bottom/last in learning, and
I don't wanna be overall bottom/last at all.

After the others have read the chapter, Mr. Harper goes back
to talking about how untrue the lives people used to live were.
We've all heard about the times before the Turn, but hearing
Mr. Harper, who is a teacher and, hopefully, not a complete
ass/idiot, talk about all the untruths people used to think were
regular makes me proud to be from now and not then. Still, I
mostly only half listen 'cause I'm thinking.

When the horn goes off and it's time for rotation, I hang
back so I can speak truth to Mr. Harper.

"Mr. Harper," I say.

"What, Ben?"

"Today, during a lot of your session, I was thinking about
beating you to death with a rock."

"Hmm, why?"

"I don't know. I'm not a brain-healer."

"If you don't know, how would I? Go to the nurse if you
want."

I walk toward the nurse's office. On the way there, I see three
shoelookers together in front of one of our school's war mon-
uments: a glass case holding a wall with the nuclear shadows
of our dead enemies on it. Two of the shoelookers cry, and the
third paces between the other two, biting his nails. Marlene is
near them. Marlene is my sibling. She is five cycles older than I
am and training to be a NumbersPlusTaxes teacher.

Marlene is also the reason I was not given a prebirth optiselection. When Marlene was optiselected, all her personality points attached to only one personality paradigm and made her a para-one, a person who's only about one thing. There are all kinds of paradigms, like intelligence, conscientiousness, or extraversion. OptiLife™ releases different personality packages people can pay for. My parents were successful enough to get a standard package of seven points to spread across a few paradigms. That's what they wanted for Marlene: a balanced, successful person. But all seven of the points that could have gone toward her being a bunch of different stuff all went to one paradigm. Ambition. And that much of anything makes you a freak/the worst. But some companies like Learning Inc. prefer people like Marlene. She is a good worker. She is good at getting things she wants. It's all she does. Get things.

When Marlene was six and I was still a crying bag of poop, my parents had to convince her that having a younger brother would actually help her to be a good teacher because she could practice information transfer on me. They also told her that I, as a clear-born, could never be in competition with her in life or their hearts after they caught her trying to smother me with a pillow. They tell that story and laugh about it now.

After Marlene, my parents decided optimizing me wasn't worth the risk. When I was younger, she used to force me to read books for hours. She tried to make me remember things, and when I couldn't, she would slap me or pull my hair or twist my fingers. When I cheated and she didn't notice, she would hug me and squeeze so tight I couldn't breathe. She'd kiss my forehead. When I got old enough to really be in school and didn't do well there either, Marlene gave up on me. "No one can make a diamond out of a turd," she said.

"Got it, Marlene," I said.

"Diamonds are actually made from—"

"I don't care, Marlene."

I'm proof she isn't the perfect teacher, and she hates me for it.

How I feel about Marlene: she could keel over plus die and I'd be happy plus ecstatic.

She has two cups of water in her hands. She looks at me quickly, then pours a cup of water onto the heads of each of the crying shoelookers. Wet the Wetter is a game people play with shoelookers sometimes. People like to trip them or pour water on the heads of criers 'cause they won't do anything back and it's humorous. The two shoelookers are crying harder than ever now but not moving. Water drips, drips from their heads and clothes.

"Ben," Marlene says. "Isn't it your lunch section?"

"Yes," I say.

"This isn't the food sector."

"I understand."

"I am inquiring because your ability to move effectively through an academic space reflects upon my own person," Marlene says. I look at the empty cups in her hands.

"I am me and you are you. I don't care what reflects on you," I say.

"You know this school will be mine in the future," she says. "Even you should understand that." Marlene always talks about how she will take the school over, how she'll be such a good teacher that everything will be hers.

"Okay. Don't talk to me," I say loudly. "Para-one," I say much more softly because she's scary. Marlene comes close to me. The shoelookers drip. The dry one paces back and forth.

"What'd you say?" Marlene asks. I don't say anything. I look at her eyes that always look the same, always searching for something to push over and stomp. Marlene backs off and lets me go. She walks away laughing at the wet shoelookers, and at me, I guess.

Shoelookers don't really do anything to anybody except make them proud to be themselves and not a no-good shoe-looker. People say that if you tell a lot of lies you eventually start being all depressed and weepy like them. The shoelookers don't feel anything but sad. They feel it so much you can see it in everything they do. They're always looking at the ground.

I walk to the nurse in big steps. Everybody gets their manda-tory Good in the mornings with breakfast at school, but they have extra at the nurse's. I go to the nurse because Good makes me feel good. When I have Good, it's easy to be proud and truthful, and ignore the things that cloud my truth, like Mar-lene, or being made into an example, or knowing I'll never be perfect.

The nurse, Ms. Higgins, is shaped like an old pear. Her body type is not attractive. She isn't in a union and doesn't have any kids because she's ugly and works as a school nurse. Today her face looks tired plus more tired. I prefer Ms. Higgins. Ms. Hig-gins looks at me, pulls her injector from her desk. There are vi-als of fresh Good on a shelf behind her.

It's quiet, so I talk. "Why don't you quit if you hate it here so much?" I ask as she screws the Good into the injector gun.

"Because I need credits," she says. She steps to me. I stretch my neck out for her and close my eyes. She puts one hand on one side of my neck. Her hand is warm plus strong. She stabs the injector needle in. My head feels the way an orange tastes. I open my eyes and look at her. She waits. I look at her more. She frowns, then gives me another shot. And then I feel the Good.

"Bye," I say to Ms. Higgins. She sweeps the air with her fin-gers, like, *Be gone.*

On the way to my usual foodbreak table, I walk past a ta-

ble of shoelookers whispering to themselves. A few are crying.
Shoelookers—if they're good for anything, it's crying. I laugh
'cause the Good is going full blast and it's funny how the shoelookers just don't have a chance. How they're so down that
even Good doesn't help them much.

At my table, Scotty, John, and some others are laughing, but
I don't know why, so I feel mildly frustrated.

"Oh, hey, Ben. We were so worried. Please have a seat,"
says John. I sit down next to him. "How are you feeling today?" Scotty asks, and I feel even more frustrated 'cause I think
they're using me for humor because I needed extra Good instead of just the mandatory breakfast Good. "We care," Scotty
says, making his voice like a bird. The table laughs. I look
around, then I relax 'cause I catch on to things, and I can see
that they're making fun of how things used to be, not me.

"Why, thank you for asking," I say. "I'm doing great." They
laugh more, and it feels great. All the laughing at the table.

"Please take my drink because you look thirsty and 'cause
you're a really smart guy," Scotty says, and everybody laughs
even harder. "Catch, Ben," Scotty says as he tosses a box drink.
I don't move to catch it fast enough 'cause I'm thinking, *I just
got Good from the nurse, and already I'm feeling things other
than good, which isn't how it works.*

The drink box goes over my hand and smacks Leslie Mc-
Stowe right in the head.

She drops her tray and her food. Leslie frowns. I laugh with
everybody else. Leslie was a twin, then her brother, Jimmy,
died. Jimmy was a shoelooker who cooked his head in a food
zapper. Leslie is always telling lies about how great things are
or how nice everyone looks and how everybody is special. Leslie McStowe is one of the least truthful people around, which is
frustrating because she and I scanned high for compatibility on

our genetic compatibility charts. Probably because we're both clear-borns. Leslie's parents have protested against OptiLife™. They don't believe in perfect. I believe in it—I just hate it.

Leslie stands there looking lost and stupid. I want more laughs, so I stand up and make my mouth a big huge smile, and say, "Sorry about that, Leslie, let me use my credits to get you a new lunch." The table goes crazy. I have a lot of credits because my mother and father are successful, which I benefit from. Leslie's face goes from *Ow* to all smiles as she looks at me. Then she says, "That's so nice of you." It's a surprising thing to hear 'cause no one has said it to me before. The table is wild/crazy, which makes me proud. I keep it going. "C'mon, let's get you another lunch," I say in a voice I imagine would have been regular a long time ago.

Leslie McStowe follows me into the food part of the cafeteria. "Those people are idiots," my mother said once. She wasn't talking about the McStowes specifically, but about a bunch of people who were giving away candy and flowers to strangers on the newscast. The McStowes and the people my mother called idiots are part of the Anti. They're anti-Good, anti–prebirth science, anti-progress. At my school I can count the number of Anti families on my hands. But there are a lot of them in worse parts of the New Federation.

"Get whatever you want," I say, even though the guys at the table can't hear me over here.

"Thanks so much!" Leslie says. When she smiles, it looks like somebody scooped holes in her cheeks 'cause of her dimples. She grabs a juice and a greens bowl, and that's it. I register my credit code into the machine for her, and she smiles at the lunch man, who doesn't say anything. "Have a great day," I say to him because I'm still doing the thing I was doing. He stares. When we come back to the main part of the cafeteria, I'm expecting a bunch of laughs. No one at the table notices. They're eating now. I feel frustrated.

"Thanks, Benny, you're such a sweetie," Leslie says. I want to let her know the whole thing was for laughs, but then I don't, because I'm thinking. I sit down, and Leslie goes to sit with the shoelookers though she herself is not a shoelooker. I think, *Maybe I should have been truthful and reminded her about the fact that her face is arranged nicely, so she would remember we scanned as compatible and might eventually be part of a workable, functional familial unit with me.*

Everybody has their own room in our housing unit. I have a mother and a father, and there's Marlene. In my room I do physical maintenance like push-ups and leg pushes, and then I read the chapters from school until I smell food. I go downstairs where my mother and father and sibling are all at a table chewing.

"What are you looking at me for?" I ask.

"I received a message saying you've been taking extra Good," my father says.

I take a bowl from the washer, and I push the button that makes the cooker front slide open. I put a spoon in. I feel the hot inside the cooker box. I fill the bowl with meat and grains from the cooker. "Sometimes I need it. And why aren't you being truthful?" I say. "Marlene told you that." Marlene, since she's training at the school, knows stuff about me and what I do there.

"Don't accuse anyone of not being truthful," my mother says.

"I obscured the full truth because you have a tendency to respond emotionally, like some kind of neck-crane," says my father. Standing and staring at them, I dive my spoon into my bowl. I take a bite and chew. The grains and meat taste like grains and meat.

"I only pay attention because people still associate me with you," Marlene says. "Once I'm certified, I won't be interested. Until then, you are still a periphery reflection of my person."

Sometimes I imagine Marlene drowning in a tank of clear water.

"Okay, I've listened to you and now I'm frustrated," I say.

"We are also frustrated because people still associate you with us even though we are our own successful individuals," my mother says.

"Not to mention the fact that your clear-birth was a mistake and that you are alive only due to your mother's irrationality brought about by maternity," my father says. My mother looks at me, then my father, and then nods her head. "It's true; it's true," she says.

I drop my food on the floor and walk away. The bowl doesn't break. The food splats on the floor.

"Have some pride, Ben," my father says.

"You always say the same things. It's frustrating," I say from the hall so they can't see me. I squeeze my eyes shut so no water can come from them. I try to have some pride. "I know I was a mistake already, so I don't know why you mention it so often."

"It's because the fact that we didn't select genes during your prebirth period almost certainly correlates to your being so slow and disappointing," my father calls. "And we're frustrated with you and tangentially with ourselves as a result."

"I know all that," I say. I go to the bathroom. I grab the house injector from behind the mirror. I go to grab a vial of Good. There is none. I spin around like it will be in the air somewhere. Then I take a breath and close my eyes and close the mirror. I open it again slowly, hoping it will be different. It

isn't. There is an injector but no Good. I want to scream but
don't. Instead, I go to my room. I sit on the bed.

I try to sleep. All I do is sweat and feel hurt all around my
body and in my head. It gets dark. By then, I feel like death/
poop. Deep into the night, my mother comes into the room.

"You've been screaming," she says.

"I don't care if I've been disturbing you; I'm frustrated you
hid our Good," I say from under the covers. I hear her step to
me; she rips the covers away. She is frowning in the dark. She
puts a hand on my face and turns it. Then she uses the injector
in her hand and stabs it into my neck. She gives me three shots,
and the Good makes my teeth rattle. My mother's hand sits on
my head for a while. Then she turns and leaves. And then everything feels so right and so fine that I fall asleep smiling.

At school I get my usual morning Good. And in HowItWas
class we talk about before again.

"So even though people said all these things and acted like
everyone else was important, there were still wars and hurting,
which proves it was a time of lies," Mr. Harper says.

"But yesterday you said some frog crap about how some
things were better and how it was easier in the old days," Scotty
says.

"This is why you'll be a midlevel tasker at best," Mr. Harper
says. "I said some people still believe that the old way was better. Some people still live the old way because they prefer it."

"I think those people are assjerks," Scotty says.

"No one cares what you think," Mr. Harper says. "Though
I agree with you."

"H-how dow know?" says Samantha in her deep, broken
voice. She is normally quiet. "Mahbe okay."

"Shut up, screw-face," Scotty says. He takes off his shoe and throws it at Samantha. It hits her and makes a thunk sound and then bounces off her head onto my desk. The class laughs. Mr. Harper laughs. Samantha tries to laugh. I stare at the shoe.

"See, here we have a teachable moment," Mr. Harper says. "Back before the Turn, Scotty might not have been honest about how he expressed himself, and Samantha would go on thinking he thought what she said was smart."

I go straight to Ms. Higgins after class. When I get there, she looks at me like I'm broken.

"You've been put on a Good restriction by your legal guardians," she says. I can see the vials behind her. I can almost feel them. Almost but definitely not.

"I only need two," I say. "Even one shot, please."

"A formal restriction has—"

"I know," I yell. I turn around and leave.

The floors of the school are tan and white. I walk to lunch. It is hard to keep my head up 'cause I don't feel proud or good at all.

When I get to the cafeteria, I hear someone say, "Happy birthday." When I look up, I see Leslie McStowe looking at me. She's sitting at a table with a bunch of sorry shoelookers. Then she stands and wraps her arms around me. "Happy birthday," she says again. I used to hide in my room and try to remember everything from whatever Marlene had given me to read so I could get a hug like that after her tests. But this is the first one I've had in many cycles. I'm standing there thinking of how Leslie McStowe is strong plus soft. I can feel her breathing on my neck a little.

"It's your birthday," Leslie says. She is smiling at me. Her eyes seem excited/electronic.

"Oh," I say. I have seen fifteen cycles now.

"We scanned compatible, you know. It's in your charts," she says quickly, answering the question I was thinking.

"Oh."

"If you want, my parents would love to have you over to celebrate." She looks down at the floor, not like a shoelooker, but like she's ashamed. "They like celebrating things."

"I don't celebrate like that or associate with you. Also, everyone thinks your parents are strange," I say.

"I know, but it would make us all really happy," she says. This, I realize, is exactly what Mr. Harper was speaking of. Leslie McStowe wants me to make her happy for no reason. I look at her and am lost in something that doesn't feel like pride or intellect or what truth should feel like. "Please," she says, and she hands me a paper that is an invitation for later in the day. I take the invitation, and then I walk to the table where I normally sit with the people I usually associate with.

At home, my familial unit says things to me.

"Hello," my father says.

"You seem agitated," my mother says.

"You are now on the Good restriction list," Marlene says.

I don't say anything to anyone. Without any Good in me, everything looks like a different kind of bad. And all I can imagine are the worst things about everyone and everything. And I can't tell if my stomach is aching or whether I'm imagining how bad a really bad stomachache might be if I had one right then. Either way it hurts. Ideas that scare me run around in my head. I go to the bathroom. I pull the mirror back. There is an injector, but there is still no Good. None. Only a shaver and fluoride paste and a small medical kit. I look in the medical kit just in case. No Good. I take the empty injector and bring it to my neck. I hit the trigger and stab and hope maybe I'll get something. I hit the trigger again. Again. I close the mirror, and a small crack appears in a corner of the glass. I go outside. I'm afraid of how bad I feel. No one asks where I am going.

The McStowes live in a complex on the outer part of the section. In our section the poor people all live on the outer parts so those of us on the inner parts don't have to come in contact with them all the time. They live cramped together in small spaces that are cheaper and, as a result, not as nice in looks or housing capabilities: keeping warm/dry, being absent of animals, etc.

I haven't had any Good since breakfast. I can feel the no-Good pressing on me. Pulling me down. It is getting dark outside. Out at the edge of the section, there are so many shoelookers slowly moving through the walk-streets. They've been abandoned by the people who used to be their families. That's what happens to most shoelookers. There are a bunch of soon-deads, and there are a few kid-youths and also every other age there is. Once in a while, one of the shoelookers will snap her head up and her eyes will be wild like she just remembered something important. Then, after a few seconds of wild looking and head turning, she'll drop her head back down.

It's worse than frustrating. Being around all those downed heads makes me want to close my eyes forever. I follow the grid-walks toward where the McStowes live. I focus on the ground because it doesn't make me want to disappear as much. The ground on the way there is gray and gray and gray. My shoes are black and gray. Good in its vial is clean/clear.

Long fingernails bite my shoulders. I look up and see a shoelooker my mother's age. Her hands are near my neck. She screams, "Where are we going?" and shakes me like she's trying to get me to wake up. Her voice is screechy like she's been yelling for a long time. I shove her, then I run because I'm very disturbed.

I make sure I'm looking up as I run. I'm sweaty when I reach Leslie's housing complex. Inside it is not nice. A bunch of cats and a raccoon race and fight in the lobby area. The walls are dirty and the paint is peeling. I walk up a stairwell that smells like a toilet. When I find the McStowe door, I knock on it. I can hear people rustling inside. I imagine myself falling into a jar of needles over and over again. I haven't had any Good. The door opens. It's bright inside.

"Happy birthday" comes out of several mouths. The voices together make my heart beat harder.

"Hello," I say.

"Come in, come in," says Leslie. There's a tall man with a skinny neck and gray hair. He wears an ugly shirt with bright flowers on it.

"Great to see you; really great to see you," Father McStowe says. I'm wondering if in the McStowes' home people say everything twice.

The food sector is a small space to the left. It smells like something good. In the main sector are Leslie McStowe, her mother, her father, and three fidgeting shoelookers about my age. They have the usual sad/dirty look. They might be from the school. I don't know. I don't look at shoelookers.

"Come in," Mother McStowe says even though I'm already inside. She is a thin woman with a short haircut. There are folds of loose skin under her neck. I come in farther. Everyone is looking at me.

"How was your walk over?" Leslie says. Her face is smiling.

"Bad," I say. "This part of the section is worse than where my unit lives."

"Well, I'm sorry to hear that," Father McStowe says. "Let's have some cake now that the man of the hour is here in one piece!" *Man of the hour.* He is talking about me.

There are two beds in the main section. There are sheets and plates on one bed so it can be a table. There are pillows arranged on the other to make it a place to sit.

"I've never had cake," I say. I haven't. It isn't something proud people eat. It makes people fat, my mother says, just like the candy the Antis hand out in the streets.

"Well, isn't that a shame," Mother McStowe says even though she is smiling. She has dimples like her daughter. "In this house we eat cake every chance we get, seems like." She laughs. And so does Father McStowe. Leslie laughs. Even one of the three shoelookers laughs a little. I can tell by how the shoelooker's shoulders jump while she stares at the floor.

"You shouldn't feel sorry for me," I say. "My housing unit is much nicer than this." It gets quiet, then the house starts laughing some more. Even though I don't know exactly why they are laughing, I'm not too frustrated.

"This one!" says Father McStowe. "A true comedian."

"What's a true comedian?" I ask.

"Joke-tellers, humor-makers," says Father McStowe. "Back in the old world, it was a life profession to make laughter. One of many interesting old-world lives."

"I don't believe that," I say, 'cause I don't.

"That's okay," says Mother McStowe, still giggling. "Let's eat some cake."

"Sounds sweet to me," says Father McStowe. He laughs, and so does his family.

We move over to the table/bed. The main sector of the housing unit has walls covered in sheets of paper with too many colors on them.

"Cake," Mother McStowe says as she walks to the food sector, "was a delicacy in the old world used to celebrate events like union-making, the lunar cycle, battle-victory, and, of course, birthdays." Mother McStowe looks for some utensil in the food sector. I look at Father McStowe and ask, "Is that the food sector your son killed himself in?" There's a clang/clack sound from Mother McStowe dropping something on the floor.

Father McStowe looks at me. He touches my shoulder. His hand is large/heavy. "You know something"—he speaks low so only I can hear him—"one of the things we like to do in this home is be careful of what we say. What you said didn't have to be said. And now you've hurt my wife. She'll be fine but—"

"Lying for others is what caused the Big Quick and the Long Big," I say.

"Maybe. Or maybe it was something else. I'm talking about thinking about the other person, ya know?" Father McStowe whispers to me. "I'm sure you have a lot of ideas about this, but it's something we try around here." He smiles and touches my shoulder again. "Let's eat some cake," he says in a big voice, a voice for everybody.

I haven't had any Good since breakfast. And here I am. In Leslie McStowe's house. Because she invited me and because she makes me think of things that aren't Marlene or optimization or being forever dumb/slow.

Mother McStowe comes back. She smiles at me as she hands me a knife big enough to cut a bunch of things. "It was tradition for birthday boys to cut the cake after the singing of the traditional birthday hymn," Mother McStowe says. She looks around quickly with wide eyes, then begins to sing. The rest of her family joins in. The shoelookers look down and up, and down and up, trying to decide what to be, and even they mumble along with the McStowes.

Happy birthday to ya, happy birthday to ya
Happy birthday, happy birthday to ya
Happy birthday, it's your day, yeah
Happy birthday to ya, happy birthday, yeah!

When they finish, Mother McStowe tells me, with her eyes, to cut the cake. The knife cuts through easily. "I forgot that, traditionally, you are supposed to make a wish before you cut into the cake," says Mother McStowe. "But after is fine, I suppose. You can wish for anything."

Of course, I wish for Good. I put one more cut into the cake, then Mother McStowe takes the knife from me, and I see she cuts into the middle of it instead of off the side like I did. She cuts pieces for everybody. Father McStowe and Leslie and I sit on the bed made for sitting. The rest stand and chew. The cake is the sweetest thing I've ever eaten.

"Do you like it?" asks Mother McStowe.

"It's good 'cause it's so sweet," I say. It makes my tongue and teeth feel more alive.

"And it's an authentic old-time recipe you can't get any- where else," Mother McStowe says.

When half my cake is gone, I turn to Father McStowe. "Do you have any extra Good?" I ask somewhat discreetly, since taking too much Good is not a proud thing. Father McStowe looks at me with cheeks full of cake.

"We like to think of our home as a throwback to an era be- fore industrial Good," he says. He swallows, then puts a hand on my shoulder, then removes it.

"I need Good."

"You're thinking now; this is then." Father McStowe does something with his hands. "Think of our home as a place where no one needs industrial Good."

"Is it because you're poor that you don't have any Good?" I ask. Father McStowe laughs so hard he spits wet cake onto the floor. Quickly, Mother McStowe cleans it up. He looks to his daughter, and says, "This one is funny. A real comedian."

"I'm not telling jokes," I say.

"That's why you're so good," Father McStowe says. "When I want to be funny, I usually tell an old-time joke, like this one." He clears his throat. "Have you heard the one about the deaf man?"

"What?"

"That's what he said!" Father McStowe says. "If you would have said no, I would have said neither has he. Get it?" He touches me on the shoulder and chuckles. Leslie and the shoe-lookers giggle with him. "Truly, we like to think we, as you've seen, have created a space that is really a throwback to a time before the Big Quick or even before the Long Big. My family and I re-create that decent era for people who might want or need it."

"I'm frustrated because you don't have any Good. I'm leaving," I say.

"What we—hey, Linda, could you grab some of our literature?—offer here is a way to feel and be happy without Good. We can feel good just by being together, and you can join us a few times a week depending on the package that works for you." Leslie is smiling, and the shoelookers are eating cake, switching between weak smiles and lost frowns.

"I'm going home," I say.

"Take some literature," he says. With her face smiling, Mother McStowe hands me a pamphlet. On it are smiling faces and words and different prices. Different amounts of time are trailed by different credit values on each row of information.

"There are lots of choices," Leslie says.

"Think it over. If any package feels right for you, let Leslie know. We recommend starting off with at least three days a week here with us in the Era. You'll feel brand-new. Just look at these guests." Mother McStowe points to the shoelookers, who are still munching cake. They look at me and they all try to smile.

I get up. "I'm frustrated because I thought this was something different," I yell. I haven't had any Good. I feel the pamphlet crushing in my fist. On the front, it says LIFE IN THE ERA in curly letters. "Also, your daughter doesn't frustrate me, so that's why I came."

"Look over the literature," Father McStowe says when I'm at the door.

"I haven't had any Good since the morning, that's why I'm emotional," I scream before I slam the door and run back to my own housing unit. I get tired, so I have to walk. Plus, there is no Good at my housing unit anyway. The night is black. The gridwalk is gray and gray and gray. There's some sweet left on my teeth, and even after the sweet is gone, thinking about it helps keep me walking.

At breakfast the next day, the Good makes me feel better for a few minutes but not even through to the last sip of my milk. My neck aches. My brain throbs. The floor of the school is mostly tan, and the patterns against the tan are at least easy to drown in. In Mr. Harper's class, we are talking about the Long Big and how it led to the Big Quick, like always. I think of cake during class.

At lunch I go to sit with my usuals. At the table Scotty says, "Back off, we don't want to associate with a shoelooker like you." Somebody else says, "Go sit with the downs over there." I just stand there looking at the ground because I'm not a shoelooker even though, with my head down, and the feeling in my head, and the tears almost in my eyes, I probably look like one.

I try to be proud and look up. I feel a boom and a hurt under my eye. I fall. The table laughs. I see that John has punched me to say I am officially not welcome. My face hurts. I want to lie there, but I get up because I'm pulled up. It is Leslie Mc-Stowe who pulls me. She is frowning. When I'm standing, I pick my head up, and she walks with me to the nurse's office. "It's okay," Leslie says, lying like they used to, like she does. And I am happy to hear her do it.

In the nurse's office Ms. Higgins stares at the two of us. Samantha is sitting in a chair. Samantha is not healthy, ever, but she looks at me, like, *Welcome,* and does her happier moaning sound. Ms. Higgins pulls a cold pack out of a cold box. I put the cold over my eye. It makes the hurt less. I sit in a chair next to Samantha. Leslie sits in one next to me.

"He got hit," Leslie says.

"Yah ohkay?" Samantha groans.

"You got hit," Ms. Higgins says.

"Yes," I say. Ms. Higgins says nothing. Then she stands up and opens the drawer that holds her injector. Hearing the drawer slide open makes my skin tingle. She turns her back to us so she can feed some fresh new Good into the injector.

Then, at the office door, I see my sibling. "I heard," says Marlene, "you've become a real shoelooker." Leslie touches my not-cold hand. Her fingers are warm on mine. "Ben is on a Good restriction, Higgins," Marlene says. With one eye, I look at Leslie McStowe, then at Samantha, then at Marlene, and then at Ms. Higgins. Ms. Higgins screws a vial of Good into the injector. "I'll report you," Marlene says.

Ms. Higgins continues screwing the vial into the injector and does not look at Marlene. Marlene stands at the office door. She's holding a cup of water. All I want is Good. Ms. Higgins looks at me with her loaded injector. Leslie squeezes my hand. I look at Ms. Higgins. I shake my head. Ms. Higgins drops her injector on her desk then sits down in her chair. She turns her head and looks at the wall. We are quiet. It's quiet for a long time. Leslie looks at me. She wants to smile, but she can't, so with my head down, one hand warm, one hand cold, one eye bruising and the other looking at her, I say, "Have you heard the one about the deaf man?"

LARK STREET

An impossible hand punched my earlobe. An unborn fetus, aborted the day before, was standing at my bedside. His name was Jackie Gunner.

"So, I guess you didn't have the balls?" Jackie Gunner said. His voice was a stern squeak. My eyelids rolled open. He was a tiny silhouette on the end of my pillow. Smaller than a field mouse.

"Well, say something, *Dad*." He said Dad the way some people say cunt. "Do you even feel bad?"

"Yeah," I said. "I feel real bad."

"*I feel real bad*," Jackie Gunner repeated. "Is real bad a hole big enough to fit our lives in?"

"Our?" I said.

"It's a metaphor, Daddy," said a new voice, this one shy, charming even. A second tiny fetus climbed up my comforter onto my bed. Her name, I knew, was Jamie Lou.

"Phew," Jamie Lou said at the summit, which was up near my pillow. She plopped down so she was sitting beside Jackie Gunner. A tiny shadow beside a tiny shadow. Twins, I thought.

"I'm sor—" I began.

"Don't," Jackie Gunner said. "Just don't.

"So you didn't have the balls, huh?" he repeated while thrusting and grabbing the space between his tiny, tiny legs. Legs that would never grow big enough to kick things like bottle caps, or soccer balls, or other people. "I think I have more balls than you and I'm still, like, a trimester from genitalia." Here he paused as if in reflection. "What are balls like?"

Jamie giggled.

I didn't know how to answer him. "Uh, they . . . well . . ." My voice still dragged from sleep.

"Whatever," Jackie Gunner said. "You wouldn't know. You didn't have the *cojones* to look."

"Be nice to Daddy," Jamie Lou said. Jackie Gunner grunted. Then he turned his tiny head and sort of looked at me sideways. "Look at me, Dad."

The night before, my girlfriend, Jaclyn, had taken a series of pills that had pushed Jackie Gunner and Jamie Lou out of her. When we found out it was an option, the take-home method had seemed like the way to go. We'd imagined it'd be more humane. The pamphlets instructed us—her—to tuck four pills in the space between her lip and gums. That way they would dissolve, and then the chemicals would find her bloodstream without the detour of her stomach. There would be vomiting. The pamphlet made that clear.

Jaclyn cried on the toilet. I held her hand in the beginning. Then she told me to leave. So I did. I listened from the living room.

"It's okay, Daddy," said Jamie Lou. At this, Jackie Gunner turned and kicked Jamie Lou on the side of the head. "Ouch," she said.

"Hey," I said, feeling like it wasn't the time for violence.

"Shut it. And it's not okay," Jackie Gunner said. "He won't even look at us."

"He's scared," said Jamie Lou, rising. She brought her head close to Jackie Gunner's head and kissed his temple.

"I don't care," said Jackie Gunner, ignoring the kiss.

After about an hour of the most honest pain I can remember hearing, Jaclyn said something I understood. "Oh, my God, it's in my—oh, my God," and I knew they'd been released. I thought I might try to hold her hand again then. But I could not. I could not look into that bathroom.

That was only about eight hours before Jackie Gunner and Jamie Lou appeared in my room.

"Look at me, Dad!" Jackie Gunner yelled.

I got up carefully, trying not to squish them or bounce the bed and send them flying. I flipped on the light switch.

Their heads were too big for their tiny bodies, which were each as thin as a pencil and a fleshy pink. Their skin was shriveled and translucent. I could see through their skulls to pea-size gray brains. Jackie Gunner's eyes were closed, but behind one of his eyelids there was just an empty socket. Jamie Lou had both her eyes, and she seemed to have working eyelids, too. Their hands and feet were partially webbed, and their scrawny legs shouldn't have been able to support their bodies. They wore a glaze of bright blood.

"Don't smile at me, Dad," Jackie Gunner said.

"Okay," I said.

"Tell me what my mom is like," Jackie Gunner demanded. "Tell us everything."

"Mommy," echoed Jamie Lou.

"She's pretty cool," I said.

"Okay?" Jackie Gunner said.

"You want to know right now?" I asked.

"Well, we don't exactly got a whole lot of time, Pops."

"We're not gonna be people," Jamie Lou explained, suddenly somber. I looked at her.

I thought of one place to start: my mother's Volvo. It did this thing where if you ever stopped all the way, the car just shut off about half the time. You'd have to rush to shift into park, then twist the key to off, and then turn it back on to get the car started again. It'd get going just fine, but the next time you stopped—lights out. Eventually, you got the hang of it, figured out all the little tricks. Like, if I shifted to neutral just as I stopped, the engine would maintain a healthy hum. Or you could just never stop: slow down early for every red light, roll every stop sign.

It was my third time driving Jaclyn anywhere. We were about five feet into the intersection, and I was still inching forward. Jaclyn pretended everything was normal. She wore an acid-washed denim jacket over a tank top and some cargo pants. "I'm sorry, I know I look crazy," she'd said as she flipped the passenger-side visor closed and deflated into the passenger seat with a sigh. She'd just gotten off of work at a store that sold things like cargo pants and acid-washed denim jackets. "You do look a little off. I wasn't gonna say anything, though," I'd said with a stupid chuckle. I knew she knew she looked fine. "Watch it," she said through a real smile. The car behind me honked. We ended up at a Chinese spot close to my place.

After we put our orders in, the man at the counter asked, "Separate or together?" Jaclyn shot out a "Together" before I had a chance to be awkward. I looked at her, and she laughed the laugh she does when she's about to win at something or is caught in a lie. "I deserve something for not mentioning the less-than-road-worthy car you got me riding in," she'd said.

"Your mom's a cool lady, I guess," I said to the twins. "We've been together for almost a year. But we'll probably go to different colleges in the fall."

"Oh no," said Jamie Lou, heartbroken.

"Oh no," said Jackie Gunner, mockingly. He used his arm to conk his sister over the head.

"Chill," I said.

"It's okay," Jamie Lou said. She wrapped Jackie Gunner in a big hug and kissed the side of his head.

Jackie Gunner did not look impressed. He turned his attention back to me. "So what?" he asked. "What about me?"

"We aren't gonna be people," Jamie Lou reminded him. Jackie Gunner ignored her.

"Me and Jaclyn—that's her name—well, me and Jaclyn did—she missed her period. We weren't very careful as far as methods," I continued. They're far too young to hear about this kind of thing, I thought. Jackie Gunner looked at me in his weird closed-eye kind of way, like he had no idea what I was talking about. Jamie Lou nodded silently. "She took a test," I said.

I spared them these details: Jaclyn and me in the drugstore. Her wiping her eyes and saying, "I look crazy" before we stepped in. The fact that the store was packed, which felt like a mean joke. How we were afraid of getting to the register. How we went to the register. How we were quietly connected, as close as we had ever been, as we averted our eyes from those of the strangers around us. How, if I had to pick, I'd say the hero of this whole thing was the young woman behind the store counter. How her brown eyes melted wide, then cooled to a thin, sharp, yet gentle seriousness when Jaclyn pointed behind her to the purple box, hung not far from the cigarettes and iPhone chargers, 99 PERCENT ACCURACY emblazoned on its top right corner. How she nodded and tossed the test into a bag so quickly I would have missed it if I hadn't been watching the whole thing with an unblinking, morbid interest.

"It was positive. The test. We talked about what to do and decided we couldn't handle it, I mean you—I mean a child, children."

Jackie Gunner responded with a grunt. Jamie Lou didn't say anything.

The blood that was slowly secreting from the twins' skin was staining my pillowcase, which they were now sitting on.

"After the test, we went to a clinic. She took the pills here. It was better that way. My mom works nights. It wasn't fun. It was hard for us," I said. It was hard for her. And me, too. "That's it basically," I said. Somewhere in the middle of it, I'd gotten scared that something was wrong and considered calling 911. It seemed impossible that anyone in the medical field would allow a human being to experience what Jaclyn went through. But I did not call 911. I drove her home in the Volvo. My mother left it home most days because she didn't think it was safe.

"Whatever," Jackie Gunner said. "I don't got all day. I wanna know what woulda happened."

"The psychic, the psychic!" said Jamie Lou.

"That's where we gotta go," said Jackie Gunner.

I was afraid they'd ask to go there. Their mother loved those kinds of places. "Okay," I said, smiling through my guilt. "Okay."

I threw on some jeans, some Chucks, a light jacket. The twins were losing their pink shine and becoming a grayish red. I understood their time was limited.

"Let's go, Dad, hurry up," Jackie Gunner said as he raised his tiny arms toward me like a toddler waiting to be scooped up. I tried not to look repulsed. I lowered my hand so they could climb up. Jamie Lou tried to hop up onto my hand in one great leap. She tripped and fell face-first into my clammy skin. "Whoops," she said. When she was settled and upright, I practiced moving while holding them. Cradling them like puddles in my cupped palm. They were cool and slimy.

"You guys gonna be okay?"

"No," they said together.

I walked, taking long, quick steps, with my left palm and the twins close to my chest. I used my right hand to shield them the way you'd guard a flame from the wind. If Jackie Gunner was afraid he'd fall out of my hand onto the concrete, he didn't show it. I felt kind of proud about that. But Jamie Lou curled into a small ball and was shaking with fear. Jackie Gunner kicked at her and said, "Baby! Baby, what a baby!" I stopped walking.

"Hey," I said. "Can't you be nice for one second? You going to be a jerk all day?"

"It's in my genes," Jackie Gunner replied.

"Very funny," I said, trying to make my voice bigger than it was. "It isn't cool. Do better."

"And you," I said, shifting my attention to Jamie Lou, who was peeking out from the ball she'd rolled herself into. "You need to stand up for yourself. Don't let anybody push you around like that. Okay?"

"Okay," Jamie Lou squeaked.

"Whatever," said Jackie Gunner.

I stared at him and tried to project a sense of disappointment. He stared back at me, and I felt the disappointment I wanted him to feel rain back all over me. I continued walking toward the psychic's place without looking back into my hand.

Jaclyn had gone to see the psychic two days before our appointment at the clinic.

I'd asked her not to go. She wouldn't listen. Then I'd asked her which psychic she was going to and when. "I'm going to that guy on Lark tomorrow afternoon—you want to come with me?" I'd told her I didn't believe in that kind of stuff. "You don't believe in anything," she'd said.

The next night she'd called me. I'd been waiting. "It was crazy!" she'd said. "He knew so much. He was, like, 'Even though you're feeling stuck, you need to do what you think is best for you,'" she'd said. "I didn't say anything about it. He just knew." I'd sighed heavy, heavy relief and felt guilty about how little guilt I'd felt in that moment. Jaclyn also said the psychic had told her that she and her significant other "didn't have a healthy channel of communication."

The psychic's place was a few minutes away. There was a sign that said LARK STREET READINGS on a door that had peeling green paint and a gold-colored knob. I reached for the door with my right hand, exposing Jackie Gunner and Jamie Lou to the wind and cold. I grabbed the knob, felt its icy cool in one hand and the twins shivering in the other. I let go of the knob, opened up my jacket, and slid Jackie Gunner and Jamie Lou into the inner chest pocket.

"Thanks, Pops."

"Thanks, Daddy."

"Once we're in there, you have to keep quiet. Okay? I'll do the talking," I said.

"Whatever," Jackie Gunner said. He didn't seem worried about being in the dark of my inner jacket. He was a pretty

brave little guy. Staring up at me, Jamie Lou closed her mouth
and puffed her cheeks like she was holding her breath before a
big dive.

There was a tiny spot of blood in my palm. I wiped it on
my jeans.

Again, I reached for the doorknob. The door opened with a
dry scrape, and together we stepped into the entryway, letting
cold air rattle a wind chime above us.

"Come in," a voice said. "Would you like some tea?"

"That's okay," I called up a carpeted set of stairs that led to
the psychic's reading area.

"How did you—" another voice began.

I was embarrassed before anything else. Then I felt like I was
sinking into the floor. The twins, tucked into my jacket pocket,
moved slowly against my chest.

"Jac?" I said.

She appeared at the top of the steps in gray sweats tucked
into these tall green rain boots and a black windbreaker that
used to be mine but was now definitely hers. I worked my way
up the stairs. We kind of stared at each other until she spoke.

"Hey," she said. "This is weird."

"Yeah." I walked the rest of the way up the carpeted stairs.
I thought that maybe I should have given her a hug or a kiss or
something, but I didn't. I didn't want to risk crushing Jamie
and Jackie. "I guess you wanted another reading?"

"I felt so much better after last time. And then I couldn't
sleep last night. I still don't feel great," she said, staring into
my eyes, watching me.

I took a deep breath. "That's what these guys are here for, I
guess," I said, looking away. We stepped into a beaded curtain
that sounded like rain as we walked through. It led to the psychic's living room, which was where he saw clients. There was

an old brown table with strange images carved into the wood: an eye that was also the sun, a body that crouched holding a hammer, a bear with wings. There was an entertainment system on one side of the room opposite a gray couch. The television at the center of the console was covered with a purple silk cloth. Another cloth of the exact same color was in the psychic's hands when he emerged from his kitchen, a space adjacent to the living/divining room. He used the cloth to hold a steaming pot by the rim because it had no handle. He had dark black hair and a nose ring.

He poured the tea into two cups that were already on a counter near the couch.

"Couple's session?" he asked.

Jaclyn shot me a look that said, *See?* "You knew we were a couple," she said. The twins wiggled.

"Please, have a seat, guys," the psychic said. We sat on the couch.

"So what will it be?" the psychic began. "Tarot? I'm doing a special deal on crystal readings if you want to try something different. And, of course, I can read your palms for five dollars," he said as he settled into a wicker chair across from us. He crossed one leg over the other and sipped his tea. He was so comfortable.

"What do you want to do?" Jaclyn said, looking at me. I kept my eyes on the psychic.

"I don't know," I said. "Maybe I'll just watch?"

"You came to the psychic this early in the morning, and now you're just gonna watch?"

"I didn't really plan on—"

"Me being here? So now you're gonna just sit there?"

Her voice was doing that thing it does. The psychic sipped his tea.

"I'll do the cheapest one, I guess," I said. Though what I thought was there is nothing he can say to help me.

"Fine," she said with a sigh. She sank farther into the couch.

"Great," the psychic said. "Is this your first consultation?"

"Yes," I said. He moved his wicker chair around to our side of the room and sat close to me.

"Okay, palms are a good place to start, I think." I offered him my left hand, still slightly red with the blood of Jackie Gunner and Jamie Lou. He rubbed it with the purple silk cloth; it was still warm from the tea's heat. He scrutinized my hand. Jaclyn hovered near my shoulder so she could see what was happening.

"Well, generally," the psychic said as he traced a rectangle around the outside of my palm, "the shape of your hand suggests that you tend to be pretty skeptical."

"Hmm," said Jaclyn.

"You're the type of dude who has a plan, and you value security," the psychic continued. I looked up at him; his eyes were still locked on my hand.

"Also, see these long fingers you've got," the psychic said as he traced the length of my middle finger. "That means you're sensitive to details and need things to be a certain way."

"Yup," Jaclyn muttered from over my shoulder.

"And this," the psychic said. There was a tumbling in my jacket. Jackie Gunner was probably bullying his sister again. "This is your life line," the psychic said. He pointed to the deep brown line closest to my thumb. I realized I was wasting everyone's time. I was worried about Jamie Lou. "The way your life line sweeps out to the center of your hand, it favors the Plain of Mars, you see, so that means—"

"Stop, please," I said. I pulled a five-dollar bill from my jeans and dropped it on the table. "I don't really feel well." It was true. "I think I'm going home." It felt like the twins were doing jumping jacks. I was worried. I brought my hand to my chest and pressed it there to still them. I tried to be careful.

"Are you serious?" Jaclyn said. "That's so rude."

"No worries. It's been a pleasure—good luck with everything," the psychic said, flattening himself into his chair.

"No. I'm so sorry; he's just stressed right now," Jaclyn said.

"Absolutely no problem, it's cool, it's cool, it's all cool," said the psychic. He sipped his tea.

"It is not cool, but thank you. He's been this way for a while," she said, trying to stab me with her eyes.

"This place is a joke, Jaclyn," I said. I stared at the psychic. "Tell her it's a joke."

"Man, I have nothing to do with you and yours," the psychic said. He put his mug down.

"Just admit it. Tell her," I said. "Tell her."

"Listen, I'm just the guy who gets up early in the morning and packs the trunk up. I help you get where you're already going," the psychic said calmly.

"What are you talking about?" Jaclyn asked.

I could feel the twins listening, wanting to be a part of this. It felt like they were trying and failing to pull themselves free. A muffled voice was coming out of my pocket, so I started shouting over it.

"I'm talking about how this psychic will say whatever you want him to say to anyone if you pay him twenty dollars in advance. This isn't the first time he's taken my money." I hoped I wouldn't have to say much more. The day before Jaclyn went to see the psychic, I'd called him and asked him to tell her everything was going to be okay if she'd just follow the plan she already had in place. I thought telling her the truth about what I'd done would make me feel like a giant. Instead, once I said it,

I felt weak, stupid, scared. "I'm sorry, Jaclyn, I'm really sorry," I said. She was sitting there. I reached for her hand. She recoiled from me in a way I can't remember her ever doing before.

"You think I'm some kind of idiot?" Jaclyn said. "You think he's the reason I did it? He didn't make any decision for me. Neither did you. I'm not—I don't understand how you could think this had anything to do with that. Are you insane?"

"No, I—" I began, but from the look on her face I could see there wasn't going to be any more discussion.

I heard a muffled "Wait" coming from my jacket pocket.

I left.

Once I was outside the psychic's place, I stopped walking and took off my jacket.

"You guys okay?" I asked. There was no answer. "Hey," I said. I put my hand at the pocket seam so they could crawl out. Jamie Lou appeared in my hand. She was gray and dry now.

"Where's Jackie Gunner?" I asked.

"He was bullying me," Jamie Lou said, her voice hoarse. She reminded me of a plucked leaf. "So I killed him," she finished.

"What?" I said. I felt the fear you feel when you've done something, anything, that you can't take back. I bent over and shook the jacket a little. A tiny gray body of ash fell out. "How could you?" I yelled.

"You did," Jamie Lou said.

"What?" I said.

"He wasn't going to be a person," Jamie Lou reminded me.

"It doesn't matter," I said. "You can't just—" I lowered Jamie Lou and Jackie Gunner's tiny body to the concrete.

"You said not to be a pushover," Jamie Lou squealed in her now coarse, broken voice. I could see she was almost out of time. "I did it for you, Daddy." She was a tiny speck on the ground near her tiny brother. Both were almost invisible against the gray of the sidewalk.

At the clinic, just before Jaclyn disappeared behind a white door to get her ultrasound, she looked back at me sitting in the waiting-room chair. She gave me this brave little half smile. Her eyes were bright from hiding tears. She wanted to make this whole thing a little less terrible if she could. And she did. And no matter how hard I tried, I'd probably never know exactly how she felt. But she made me feel like, as she looked back at me, maybe it was all just what it was and not the apocalypse.

"Do you hate me?" Jamie Lou said.

"No," I said.

"So you loved us, Daddy?" Jamie Lou said, hugging my shoelace.

"No," I said. I raised my foot, shook her off, and started to walk away, hoping she would not follow me.

"What are you doing?"

I turned and saw Jaclyn. She ran up to where I'd left Jamie Lou and picked her up along with the body of her brother.

"Hey," I said, walking toward her, feeling trapped and wondering if I would ever escape any of this. I wanted to pretend it hadn't happened, but I was reminded by everything I felt. "I'm sorry. I feel like, like there's only wrong answers."

"You don't care, Daddy," Jamie Lou said. Jackie Gunner, who'd been limp, was now moving very slowly in Jaclyn's hand. "Thanks, Mommy," Jamie Lou said, snuggling against Jaclyn's thumb.

"I feel like you think I don't care," I continued. "And I do care, but I was afraid that if I cared that way you'd change your mind."

"It's all right," Jaclyn said to Jamie Lou.

"You've met already?" I asked.

"Of course we have," Jaclyn said. "What did you do to him?" she asked, looking at Jackie Gunner.

"It wasn't my fault," I said. This had been my personal mantra for some time now.

"Of course it wasn't," Jaclyn replied. She took a step closer and stared me in the eye. Disappointment rained. Then she looked at our unborn children withering away in her hand. "It's fine, I'll handle it," she said with only a small fraction of the sharpness she could summon. She turned and started walking.

"Can I help?" I said.

"Maybe later," Jaclyn said, her voice tired but without malice. I watched her, then I started in the opposite direction. I walked, hoping I'd see her smile again. At home I fell asleep on a pillow stained with blood.

THE HOSPITAL WHERE

think I will go to the hospital. My arm is paining me." My father's voice. I heard him from some shallow corner of a quiet, hateful sleep. I imagined waking up somewhere different. I opened my eyes and was not somewhere different. I had no command over this place or the people in it. And yet, for the first time in more than three weeks, I felt the mark of the Twelve-tongued God, an X followed by two vertical slashes, burning on my back. My muse, my power, was awake again.

"What?" I asked.

"Can you drive?" my father asked.

"Okay," I said. I got ready. My father sat on a white plastic chair in the kitchen near the microwave and the hot plate. The only ways we had to cook. Beneath his leather sandals was a thin puddle of water that had leaked, as it did every day, from the shower in the adjacent bathroom. It was a basement. Dark mold had to be attacked with bleach regularly. But it never died. I hated this place we lived in and had for a very long time. My father scooped oatmeal into a bowl.

"Arm pain can be linked to other problems," he said. I tried very carefully to tie my shoes. "Better for you to drive." This was all long before we knew of the cancer nesting in his bones.

"You'll be fine," I said.

"I know, but just in case," he finished through a mouthful of oatmeal. While I waited for him to eat, I grabbed the latest issue of a small journal of stories and poems called *Rabid Bird* and one of my notebooks. The Twelve-tongued God beckoned in the form of the heat I felt on my back, and while I waited for my father to finish his oatmeal, I tried, finally, to write. I scribbled and felt the free feeling of fire in my bones. Transported into a world where I had command and anything was possible.

"All right, let's go," my father said too quickly. I closed my notebook and followed him outside. The drive was long and tired. My father explained to me what the doctors had told him when he'd called earlier. Essentially, he was now old enough that anything could be a big deal. They told him where to go while his normal hospital underwent renovations. We crossed the bridge. There was a spot pretty close. My father got out of the car and went into the hospital. "I'll find you," I said. I straightened the car out, then fed the meter. I walked toward the entrance thinking, *Remember this: the first time you drove a parent to a hospital.*

"What are you looking for?" said a woman who I hoped knew I was already lost and scared. She stood in front of me in purple scrubs and colorful nurse-type shoes. Her brown hair was spun into something that let everyone know she was very busy and hadn't slept in a long time. The tone of her voice, spiced with the Bronx, said I was one of many inconveniences in her life.

"I'm looking for my dad; he just came through here a second ago."

"Is that all?" She tapped her clipboard with a pen. "What

department?" I had no idea what department my father was looking for, so I told her the truth about that. "Well, I don't know how you don't know, but—" She was about to take great pleasure in telling me that I was in this situation due to my own incompetence and that even though she could not help me, she herself was very competent. I walked away from her before she could finish.

Down the first hallway and to the left was a room that looked like the main lobby of a hotel. At the front desk was a computer and two empty seats. A woman in a suit and badge was pacing back and forth in front of the desk.

"Hi, I'm looking for my dad," I said.

"Well, there's a whole lotta dads in this place," the security guard said.

"He probably just came by asking questions, too. Black guy. I'm sure he just came down this way."

"Check in emergency—that's where I've been sending everybody who doesn't know where the heck they're going." She paused so I could be certain she was ridiculing me. "You're gonna go down this hall, make a left the first chance you get. You'll be in radiology. Then walk straight through there and make another left, and you'll basically be there. You'll see."

"Thanks so much," I said.

Soon I was staring at a small entryway sign that read RADI-OLOGY I. In the hall there was an extremely old man in a wheel-chair. He groaned steadily. His white skin looked stretched and spotty. It seemed someone had forgotten him or maybe was us-ing him to prop open the door. There were so many tubes going in and coming out of him that I couldn't imagine where they began or ended. I walked past quickly. Farther down the same hall, a black guy in a wheelchair stared in my direction with eyes so empty I thought they might suck something out of me.

I made a left, then saw a pair of double doors. A lot of healthy, able-bodied people talk about how much they hate the hospital. I've said it, too, I guess.

White coats and scrubs power walked in all directions. To my right was a family of six or seven. I imagined them Italian. It seemed they were waiting on news that everyone already knew was going to be bad. They clung to one another. They pointed frustrated looks at their shoes.

"Dad," I said as I stepped through the double doors. My father looked at me, then returned to arguing with an attendant seated behind a lectern in the corner of the emergency room. "I called and was told I could meet with someone since my doctor isn't in. And now I am here, and they are telling me to wait in the emergency room. They told me to come right away." My father was speaking the way he did to a rude waiter or a careless cashier.

"I'm sorry, sir, I don't know who you called. Things are a little hectic today. Please sign the sheet," said the attendant.

"I have." My father did one of his I'm-smarter-than-you laughs. "Already signed."

"Then please wait like everybody else." It was unseemly for anyone who wasn't about to die right that second to make any kind of scene in the emergency room is what he was trying to say.

"Dad," I said. "Just wait." My father stopped and looked visibly calmer. He sat. I gripped my notebook and the journal. I felt the mark tingle on my back. "Can you call again?" I asked.

"I have already. Doctor Koppen isn't in, and now they don't know how to direct me to another doctor. Imagine!"

"I'll go back and see if I can find some kind of directory,"

I said. What I wanted to do was sit and reread a story called "Free Barabbas" from the latest issue of *Rabid Bird*. It was pretty good, the story. I was especially interested in it because it had won a contest I had also entered. I'd received an email saying that though they'd loved my submission, "Does Anybody Want a Kitten?" I was still a loser. My story was about a family and all the things that happened to them and their new kitten: sometimes the kitten is hiding under the new bed, sometimes the kitten is sick, other times it's not and the family just appreciates its furry innocence. At one point the kitten runs away, and the family thinks their new home will never feel the same again.

The winning story concerned a guy who, in his own roundabout way, confronts his past through a series of events in his old neighborhood. It wasn't so much what it was "about," but rather the way the narrator was so funny and so mean and, somehow, so honest, that made it an awesome story, the kind you don't forget. It also happened to be nothing like anything I could ever write.

In "Does Anybody Want a Kitten?" the kitten eventually comes back, but she's pregnant.

The sick feeling growing in my throat matched the burning on my back. It was a warning. My time was running out. The Twelve-tongued God had promised me I would make our lives better. That I could use the power it had granted me to change things. It wouldn't matter what I did if my father wasn't there to see what I'd done.

I got up. I left my father sitting in his brown coat with his hands on his lap. I hoped he wouldn't ask me where I was going. He said nothing. Through the double doors, the eyes of the Italian family jumped up at me. Their eyes held something

I would normally take as a look of pity, but then and there, I'm not sure what it was.

I walked back through radiology. The black guy was still there, alone. The other man, the one strangled by tubes and age, was also still there, but now he was wearing a Mets cap. I felt certain someone was using him as a hat rack. In the front lobby, the security guard looked nervous, then tough, when I approached.

"Is there, maybe, a directory kind of person? Or someone who can help me find which department I'm supposed to be in?" I asked. I pointed to the empty chairs behind the lobby desk. "Is someone going to be sitting in one of those seats soon?"

"Not today, nobody's coming. But if you don't know the department you need, then you probably wouldn't get much help anyway."

"When people come in and are trying to figure out where to go, who do they usually speak to? My dad called and he spoke to someone who told him to come in, but now that we're here, we can't figure out where to go. He normally goes to River-head, but they transferred him here."

"Who did he speak to?"

"He says her name was Martha."

The security guard almost smiled. "Just Martha?"

"Yes. I'm just wondering, if we call this hospital who are the people we would speak to? Who would help us?"

"There's a lotta phones in this hospital. You're better off going to the emergency room."

The security lady adjusted her pants and made a sound. "Thanks so much," I said, and walked back the way I came.

The *XII* on my back burned. I would have to write in the emergency room.

I sat next to my father. I quickly explained that in terms of guidance this hospital was not going to help us. My father shook his head and muttered something about how this would never happen at his usual hospital. I opened my notebook. Quietly, I prayed to the Twelve-tongued God. I looked around. Across from us was someone so old they didn't really have a gender anymore and a Hispanic woman about my father's age. I noticed a puddle beneath her seat. I didn't know what the liquid was. Seeing it in the emergency room made me feel queasy. It could have been water.

"What are you writing?" my father asked. I looked up from my notebook.

"I don't know," I said. Which was the truest thing anyone had ever said. It was still new for me to write in front of my parents—or anyone. It felt like announcing I was running for some huge office as a Green Party candidate.

"Well, what is it about?" My father turned toward me and winced as he did. "You write a lot now. What do you write about?" His curiosity stunned me. I also really had no idea how to answer.

What I could never tell my father was that I'd given myself to the Twelve-tongued God. It had happened many years before. We'd been in a house that the bank would soon want back. The nights were dark because the gas and electric company had decided enough was enough. I'd learned that many of the things I loved, the comforts that made me feel good about myself, could disappear very slowly and also suddenly. I'd learned to hate then. To hate others for having things, to hate myself for not. One day, like an angel, the Twelve-tongued God emerged from the midnight black around me, as mysterious and vital as my own breath.

"I can give you new eyes. Eyes that will work, that won't cry. I can put your hurt to use," Twelve-tongue said. "I can give you what you want." After every other word, it pulled off a mask to reveal yet another beautiful new face. Its voice sounded like every voice I'd ever heard speaking at once. "I can give you the power to be anywhere. To heal the world. To own time. To turn lies to truth. To make day into night and night into day." I nodded viciously. "You will have the power to change everything, to make the life you want."

"What do I have to do?" I asked.

"You are not yet ready," said the Twelve-tongued God, revealing a new mask, one that wore a deep frown and jubilant eyes. Then it disappeared.

I waited. After we lost the house, we spent a year cramped into a small apartment. Then we were displaced again.

The night I saw another pink eviction notice, I prayed to that mysterious being that had found me those years before. Twelve-tongue appeared again in the basement we called a home. It smiled and frowned and laughed and cried. It stood in front of me. I watched it closely. As if to impress me, it winked and where before there had been a hot plate now there was a stainless-steel oven and range. The god laughed and the hot plate was back, the range gone.

I begged on my knees for its power.

"Serve me and you will live in a different world forever."

"I'll do anything," I said. I could feel the skin on my back beginning to sear. I could smell my own burn.

"Then prove it." The Twelve-tongued God opened its mouth and reached a hand in. From its throat, it pulled out what looked like a human hand but was actually the hilt to a sharp blade, the edge growing from the hand's middle finger.

"Please," I begged. The god watched me closely; the face it wore had an insane smile and drowning eyes. It held the knife and stared at me. Then it stuck its tongue out and quickly cut it off. I watched its bleeding mouth.

"Fo eve," said the Twelve-tongued God, a new tongue growing in its mouth. "You wi ver be the same."

"Please," I begged again. The god handed me the blade. I stuck my tongue out and placed the sharp edge near my bottom teeth. I pulled up and screamed. My tongue fell, and the Twelve-tongued God reached down and snatched it before it could hit the floor.

"The pact is made," the Twelve-tongued God said, and it stuffed its own newly cut tongue into my mouth. I wish I could share what it was like to feel the new tongue weaving into my flesh. I felt the Roman twelve brand into my back. Suddenly, I could see in the dark. Day became night. I felt free.

"Thank you," I said.

"We'll see," the Twelve-tongued God said as it popped my old tongue into its mouth and chewed. Then it disappeared.

That night I wrote my first story. I saw I was chained to the new power. I had to stay with the story. Work it harder and harder until it was something greater than I could have imagined. From that day forward, I prayed to Twelve-tongue every night and every morning, asking for more tongues. For sharper tongues. When I didn't write, my brand pulsed and ached. When I wrote badly, it screamed fiery chords. But then, when I made sentences that lived, it quieted and I could feel my ability growing. Still, I craved more tongues, new worlds to live in, and more power to change the one I was in now. I loved it. It was very lonely.

———

A nurse called out sounds that we both understood as her attempt to pronounce our last name.

"What kind of stories do you write?" my father asked again.

"It's about a guy who's hurt, I guess," I answered.

"Oh, that could be interesting," my father said. This was the most we'd ever discussed my writing.

"I don't know," I said. Someone attempted to call our name again. My father looked at me, then got up. He left his long coat on the seat beside me. I scooped the mess of brown cloth onto my lap.

"I'll wait here," I said.

My father didn't say anything before he disappeared through the double doors.

I exhaled. I closed my notebook and sat back in the emergency-room chair. I pressed my eyes shut. I could hear the quiet chatter of the healthy and sick.

After a while, I opened my eyes. A couple came in supporting each other with interlocking elbows. I couldn't tell the afflicted from the crutch. They found a seat in the room's corner near the attendant and his lectern.

"Did you ever find your mother?" The nurse I'd seen when I'd first entered the hospital was standing in front of me. I remembered her color-splashed scrubs and shoes.

"It was my dad, but yeah," I said. The nurse smiled.

"Was it? What if it was your mother?" the nurse said. She winked once with her left eye. Then she winked again. I looked down. My father's coat was gone. In its place was a black coat with a flourish of black sequins. It smelled lightly of a fruity perfume.

"No," I said. "It's my father. It is my father I'm waiting for."

"Fine," said the nurse. The Bronx accent waned, and a voice that could be anything took its place. "At least you know that much." I was again holding a brown trench coat that smelled like talcum powder and sweat.

I stared at the Twelve-tongued God, overjoyed and afraid as usual.

"Why now?" I asked. "Why now?" I wanted to yell but didn't.

"Don't be silly," said the Twelve-tongued God. She put her stethoscope in her ears, reached over my shoulder, and pulled my shirt up. She pressed cold metal on my mark. Since I'd first gotten it, the mark had grown and evolved. Around the *XII* was a dark mural of shadow figures and words I couldn't understand. "You're the one who's neglected me; I wasn't even sure it was you." The Twelve-tongued God smoothed my shirt back down, then pinched my cheek.

"I've been trying," I said. My fists were clenched.

"Really," said the Twelve-tongued God. She reached down and unclenched my fists. "Are you really trying?"

"You have no right to—"

"I am the right to," the Twelve-tongued God said. "Aren't I the one who made you something? Or maybe you'd rather cook on a hot plate for the rest of your life?"

"No," I said. I was on the verge of tears. The Twelve-tongued God sighed deeply. I was, um . . . a burning pulled at the corners of my eyes. "It's not easy for me. I need more from you. I need more tongues. I'm not good enough yet. I want to go all the way."

"Then go all the way," the Twelve-tongued God said to me. "Make what you want to see." The Twelve-tongued God reached down and kissed me on the forehead. "Really?" said the Twelve-tongued God.

I focused. I imagined what I wanted and what should be. And as I did, I saw that actually, no, the Twelve-tongued God hadn't kissed me on the forehead. That didn't happen. Instead, she grabbed me by the face and pressed a long hard lick up my neck, stopping at my ear. It felt warm and wet, like so many good things. My *XII* glowed and pulsed. "Don't be boring," the god said as she started to leave. I wanted to ask, *When will I be a winner?* And though the thought never reached my throat, the Twelve-tongued God turned to me just before disappearing through the double doors, and said, "When you win something."

I felt the power of the Twelve-tongued God spinning in my gut, looking for a place to go. I got up, carrying my father's coat in my arms. I needed to feed the meter. I wanted to check in with my father but realized he'd left his cell phone in the jacket. I sighed. Then I remembered that there were people around me who might not see their loved ones ever again. I walked out through the double doors.

The Italian family was still there, though I could tell that since I'd seen them last they'd either heard the terrible news they'd been anticipating or that the lack of any news at all had finally broken them. One woman in the family was crying into another's chest while a younger man rubbed both of their shoulder blades. I slipped by them quickly. If there was a ticket, it would be my fault.

The old men in radiology were as forgotten as ever. I made a point of noticing the old white guy exploding with tubes and the empty-looking black man because I felt like their not giving me anything meant I was to forget them, and I did not want to forget them yet.

The security guard who took pleasure in not helping me was adjusting her belt and strolling along a tiny circle. Outside, it was alive and sunny in stark contrast to the hospital, which was bright but dead. There were people walking around everywhere. None of them had any idea that maybe my father was sick and damaged. I swapped the old ticket for a new one. Adulthood is paying the meter on time, I thought. I walked back toward the emergency room.

Inside, the security guard was now arguing with a woman in a tight suit who seemed to want to make a show of things. I was happy to see angry people.

Back in radiology, the old men were still dying. I continued to the emergency room. On the way, the colorful nurse walked by; she yawned into her clipboard then looked at a watch on her wrist. I tried and failed to make eye contact.

The Italian family was with a doctor now. They huddled around him, as if he were a quarterback explaining the face of the next down. I stood away from them. Nurses and doctors rushed around. Trying to help when, really, what could they do? From the looks of things, that's what the doctor was telling the family: he wasn't a miracle worker despite the white coat and the machines. Then, suddenly, he rose up out of the huddle and pointed at me. He said, "That young man there can end your suffering. He is putting you through this. Maybe for no reason at all. He doesn't know why, and he doesn't even have the heart to end it. He's just going to—" I pretended I didn't hear the doctor say anything and continued back into the emergency room. I felt Twelve-tongue's hand like hot oil washing over my back. I wanted to tell the family that they mattered and weren't just grim decor. I didn't know how to tell them that, so I sat down and opened my notebook and tried to direct the fear and fire I felt in my body onto the page.

I looked up from the notebook.

Another older woman was coming in with what had to be her husband. They'd been together so long they were basically

twins. The same hunched backs and thick glasses and droop-
ing, tired faces. She used a blue rolling walker. I tried to ignore the couple and think. The old lady with the walker told
the woman at the information window she'd been feeling very
faint for the last three days. I could see that she and her husband were pretending they didn't know the "faintness" was her
soul stretching out before a great marathon.

Is the family of —I heard something like my last name over
the screeching PA system and decided it must be my turn to
speak with the lady at the information window.

"Hi." I told her my name and that I was the son. I smiled
at the old couple. That was my way of pretending with them.

"Do you have your father's insurance information?" the
woman at the window asked.

"I don't," I said. "I can go find him and get it," I added
quickly. "But I'm not sure where he is, exactly."

"He should be in bed fifteen," the woman said. "Just down
the hall."

"Fifteen?" I asked. "Like, he's in an actual bed?" I could no
longer pretend I wasn't afraid.

"Bed fifteen," she repeated.

As I passed the Italian family, I put my notebook, the journal, and my father's coat down and did a cartwheel to show
them that kind of thing was still possible. They looked up at
me, unamused. Then they returned to their sorrowful hugs and
mutterings. I picked my stuff back up. I found my father wearing a dotted hospital gown. He'd spent most of his life in a tie.
We stared at each other for a while. There were beeping sounds
everywhere. He was carving out the last of a cup of Jell-O.

"They gave you food?" I asked.

"Well," my father said. "I was hungry."

"So what's happening? I need your insurance stuff." My father asked me to find his pants, which were somewhere beneath his hospital bed. I pulled two cards from his wallet and waited for him to answer me.

"I'm still waiting for the—well, there she is now."

The colorful nurse trotted toward us in a way that made me uneasy. She rubbed the back of my neck as she walked by me.

"Is this your son?" the Twelve-tongued God said to my father.

"Yes, can't you tell by how handsome he is?"

"I can, I can," said the Twelve-tongued God. She winked at me and I saw diminished blood cells, emaciation, chemotherapy, hair loss, diapers, more chemotherapy, fading fathers and heartsick sons grabbing, grabbing with weak hands for anything. Words that tried to make something pretty out of shit. "You must be wondering what's going on?" the god continued.

"We are," my father said. He laughed weakly.

"Okay, it looks like"—the Twelve-tongued God seemed to be looking at her clipboard, but she peered over the edge— *nothing is more boring than a happy ending,* her eyes said. I stared back and tried not to flinch from the gaze of my creator. I took a deep breath.

"Your blood pressure was a little higher than we'd like, so we checked that out, but other than that, everything looks great. After you give them your information, you'll be free to go." The Twelve-tongued God smiled at my father, then looked at me with a face both bored and disgusted.

Once my father was dressed, we began to walk back to the emergency room to handle his paperwork. "I can do it," I said. "You go back; the meter's almost up."

"Okay, good idea," he said, and disappeared in the direction of radiology.

For what I hoped would be the last time, I walked by the

grieving family. I stepped into their family circle. The pain in my back, the fire of the *XII*, made it difficult to walk. I spoke clearly. "Whoever you think you've lost is not lost. Go home." They looked at me like I was a static-garbled television. "Go home, whoever it is, they're alive and well."

"How?" a woman said.

"It just is. They just are. Strange miracle. And now you've realized the power of family bonds. Everyone wins."

"It's so unlikely," said a man, who I assume was some kind of uncle. "Feels almost cheap?" he said, grinning despite himself.

"Well, yeah," I said. "It is what it is."

The colorful nurse walked by. "Coward!" she screamed at a nearby doctor. I skipped into the emergency room. All of the broken people there groaned and groaned. I made my voice big and announced to the masses, "There's been a great miracle. None of you are hurt. Go home." They looked up at me and blinked. Some smiled weakly, but none moved.

"Please be decent," the attendant hissed. He looked at me with pleading eyes.

"Please, sir," said the clerk at the window who needed my father's insurance information.

"Here you go," I said, and threw the insurance cards at her. She stared at me, and then went to pick the cards up from the floor. While she was bent over, I leaned over the threshold and punched the intercom. I spoke into it, and my voice flew all over the hospital. "You are all healed. Go home. This is the hospital where sickness ends. Everything will be fine, and you are happier than you've ever been. Leave. Everyone is good. Especially you."

"Sir," the attendant said. But I was already running toward radiology. The tube-tied old man was very, very slowly pulling himself free of the plastic. The other man was also sitting up, eyes opened and locked on me. I felt my *XII* like it was a new brand.

"That's it," I said. "Go forth and be healed. I'm trying to help you." I was happy. As happy as a sunflower in a field of other less radiant sunflowers. The man with tubes crawled to the edge of his bed, then fell flat on his face toward the tile floor. I screamed, "No." And the man, dislodged finally from all the tubes, froze in the air, a weightless icon, a displaced swimmer who waded in the open air. With great effort, he looked up at me as he floated. "This is the hospital where the affliction is flight," he said. Then he returned to the call of gravity and fell hard back down to the ground.

He did not move once he was there. The other man never took his eyes off me. "This is that place," he said.

I ran away toward the entrance. A sea of hospital-gown-wearing humans surrounded the security guard. She tried desperately to direct groaning patients back to wherever they belonged. She caught my eye and scowled as I ran by.

"Please, no running," the security guard yelled.

Outside, my father was sitting in the driver's seat. I was relieved to be a passenger. From all the entrances and exits of the hospital, hobbled, hurt people were emerging. They were mostly old, anywhere else they'd be untreatable, and still they made their way out into the sunshine. The affliction is flight, I thought with a hazy focus, the only kind I could muster with the exploding pain I felt in my back. And suddenly, just as they stepped through the threshold into the outside, the old sick bodies rose into the air and floated a few inches above the ground; there they hovered, weightless, immaculate, wearing thin hospital gowns and colorful socks. They were in the air for almost ten seconds, taking careful steps forward before they fell back to the earth. Their ankles gave out immediately. On the ground, they crawled like babies, if they moved at all. More stepped forward, flew, then fell. It kept happening. It kept happening. I turned to my father.

He stared at all the people flooding and floating out of the hospital. He shook his head and said, "What have you done?"

"It's about a hospital where people can fly," I said.

"What have you done?" he begged.

ZIMMER LAND

Welcome to Zimmer Land," Lady Justice says.
  I flash my ID badge at Mariam. She frowns at me from her chair in the front box office.

I use the employee entrance behind Lady Justice—all thirty feet of her. When it's quiet, you can hear the gears that move the huge scale she's holding up and down. The sword she has in her other hand is longer than my body, and it points directly at you when you're at the ticket booth.

I sprint to Cassidy Lane, a cul-de-sac module with working streetlights and automated bird chirps.

When I get to the back door of house 327, the fourth house on the lane, I'm sweaty, which I can work with. The bathroom in house 327 is the primary player's changing room. There's a timer above the toilet that lets the primary player—me most of the time—know when patrons expect to start getting their justice on. Two minutes. I strip down to my briefs, then I put on my armor. We use outdated versions of the exoskeleton battle suits that the marines use. I start with the mecha-bottoms: a pair of hard brown orgometal pants that make me limp before they're activated. Once they're activated, I can squat a half ton. Once I have the mecha-bottoms on, I jump into baggy jeans. Then I latch into my mecha-top—two orgometal panels that snap together over my chest and back. It feels like a skin-on-skin hug that doesn't stop. With my top secure, I open a pack of stretchy white tees. There are three in the bag; I'll go through at least two bags this shift. I throw on boots, and I put on dark sunglasses to protect my eyes. I take a deep breath. The mirror in the bathroom is two panels. I check myself out on one side, make sure I look the part. The other panel is a large receiver screen that shows me the inside of house 336 and the patron/patrons I'll soon be introduced to. I tighten my belt. I touch my toes and swing my arms a few times. The last thing I do is grab what looks like a skinny joint but is actually the remote to activate the mecha-suit.

I locate myself in Cassidy Lane's primary player: a young man who is up to no good or nothing at all.

I tuck the trigger/joint behind my ear as the buzzer goes off. I watch the screen.

The patron looks like he's in his forties. He's kind of fat with reddish hair and wearing jeans and a T-shirt. He sits on a couch. He has an orange bracelet on his wrist, which means he's signed the waiver for full contact. Green means I can't touch them. Orange means I can engage the patron with reasonable and moderate physical contact to enhance the module's visceral engagement. Green or orange. I don't know which patrons are worse.

The induction process begins: in house 336, a voice like warm gravy comes in through speakers shaped like books on a bookcase: "Welcome to Cassidy Lane, your home, your safe place." The voice recaps how the patron has performed to that point, explaining everything in a tight little narrative that covers whether or not they succeeded in identifying who was stealing money at the Work Jerk module, how amazing it was when they stopped that terrorist plot during the Terror Train module (if they chose to pay an additional $35), and how now, finally, they can go relax, safe at home. That is until . . . the voice tremors with worry. "What's this? It seems today isn't just any day on Cassidy Lane." Then an automation sends the blinds shooting open as if the house is possessed by a poltergeist. "He's here again. The stranger. You've seen him walking around. Wandering closer and closer to your home. This week, you're the head of the neighborhood watch. Maybe it's time you asked him a few questions." A chime goes off. Three holes in the wooden floor open and up pop three different pedestals. Pedestal A has a holophone that could be used to call the cops, family members, or anybody else. Pedestal B has a gun (a BB gun that sounds and looks like the real thing). And pedestal C is empty. It's for the tough-guy patrons. Almost all patrons (84 percent when I've been on the module) grab the gun on pedestal B. Almost nobody uses the holophone. "Remember, this is your home, not his." And then it begins.

I go outside, breathe in the fresh air, then loiter. I stand around and do nothing. I look at my phone, and once in a while I touch the joint behind my ear. And then I walk down the street slowly.

The patron opens his door.

He's not smiling. The engagement protocol on the lane is response through mimicry. If he's not smiling at me, I'm definitely not smiling back at him.

"Aye, buddy," the first patron of the day says to me. I look at him like he is looking at me. Eyes squinting, jaw clenched.

"Hey, buddy," I say from the sidewalk. He's in the street, coming toward me.

"I got a question for you," he says, kind of jogging toward me.

"That's all right," I say. And make to walk away.

"Now you wait just a second. I want to know what you're doing here."

"What are *you* doing here?" I ask. The patron's cheeks get red. Then his chest puffs out. He steps up onto the sidewalk so we can be about the same height.

"I live here. This is my home. I belong here."

"So do I," I say.

"You still haven't answered my question. What is it you're doing here?"

"You haven't answered my question either," I say.

He moves his head to look around, then focuses back on me. "I just did. I live here. That's what I'm doing. Living. Now what are you doing?"

"Same," I say. "Living." Then I turn my back to him to keep walking away.

"You listen to me. I don't want any trouble. I'm asking you a simple question." He raises his voice, so I do, too.

"I'm not answering any of your questions," I say, turning back to look at him. His hands hover near his waistline.

"Then I'm gonna have to ask you to get on outta here."

"You in charge?" I ask. "You're the boss of the world?"

"To you I am. Now fuck outta here."

"What?" I say.

"I said get the fuck outta here!" the patron says. He's screaming at me.

"I'm not going anywhere," I say without raising my voice, ignoring engagement protocol.

"Listen, I don't want any thugs out here. You have to go."

I march a little circle around the man and laugh. "I'm going to do what I want." His fist catches me under the ear, and it makes me shuffle back. He knocks the glasses off my face. I don't usually get caught so off guard. I grab the joint behind my ear and put it in my mouth. I bite down on it, and the pressure triggers mecha-suit activation. The orgometal on my legs and chest expands, and I can feel it synching to my body. The orgometal hugs me tighter, and soon I can't tell where the machine starts and the human begins. Everything gets easier. Activating the suit feels like stepping out of water into open air, like freedom. I had to do a week of training in the suit to get certified to use it.

"Fuck you," I say, and it's easy to be a convincing actor. The orgometal makes the pants that were baggy tight. Same for my shirt. I become a huge block of muscle. Something different, more dangerous than a man. My head hurts. The patron's eyes go wide for a second. I locate: I'm a kid hit by a stranger. Instead of his face, I punch a car that's in a driveway near me. The metal folds around my fist. Then I walk toward him. I take two steps. He points the handgun at me. I locate: your life is in the hands of someone who doesn't even know you and thinks you don't deserve it.

"Wait," I say. He shoots. Faux bullets explode on my chest. The mecha-suit is tweaked so pouches of red blood from one of four pockets burst on any high-velocity impact. I have to replace the blood pouches in the pockets every four walkthroughs.

What's left to do? I charge. My stomps are heavy and huge. He shoots again. I make sure I'm close enough that when the pouch explodes warm what-would-be blood gets on the patron's face. He's breathing hard, and Murderpaint™ faux blood is sprinkled on his face, and he's forgotten that he paid to be here with me. I touch the patron's neck with my orgometal-enhanced hand. He pulls the trigger again. His shirt gets drenched. It looks almost like he's the one who's been shot. I cough a death cough, and then I fall at his feet. I make *oh, ahh* sounds. The patron looks down at me. *Pop* goes the gun a final time. I can barely feel the shot hit my chest because of the suit. I'm quiet, dead, with my eyes open, staring into the sky/the patron's eyes, staring right into his human. The patron runs to house 336, then back to my body. He picks up my glasses, then puts them down, wipes them off with his shirt. He's scared and thrilled. After exactly three minutes of the patron's not knowing what to do, three minutes of his thinking about taking my pulse, then thinking better of it, three minutes of his making a sound I always hope is the thing before real honest tears but is often just panicky breath, sirens go off. Saleh and Ash, playing cop #1 and cop #2, drive into the lane. They jump out of the car and sound very stern as they ask the patron what happened.

"He attacked me!" the patron says. "He tried to kill me." I keep my eyes dead and continue to shallow-breathe. According to the guidelines, he's to be brought into the second part of the module, the Station, for a brief questioning, after which he'll be emailed a complimentary story about how he was found innocent in court after claiming self-defense. When Saleh and Ash take the patron away, I lie on the concrete for another minute before getting up. Then I press a release trigger near my belly button to disengage the mecha-suit. I go to change my shirt and wait for the next patron.

When patrons leave and fill out their postmodule surveys —which have a rating ranging from one, meaning not at all, to five, meaning absolutely—they mark five all through the questionnaire if I was on the clock. Did they have fun? *Five.* Did they viscerally feel justice was at work? *Five.* Would they come again? *Five.* In the comments section they write things like, "I'll be back soon. I'd bring my kid if I could."

I do six more walk-throughs that morning. I don't really feel like eating with anyone on my lunch, so I stay in my dressing room. Normally, I eat with Saleh, and we joke about how much we hate working, but she's been picking up more walk-throughs at the Terror Train, so I stay in the dressing room until it's time to go get shot some more. Then I clock out.

I wave to Mariam, and say, "That's my time," and she punches me out.

Once I made the mistake of getting into my car when the protesters were out in the lot. Since then, there's some kind of thing waiting for me at the end of every other shift. Sometimes it's eggs on the window with not-nice things drawn into the splattered yolks. Today, I see too many papers to count windblown and scattered in the area around my car. A bunch of them are stuck under the windshield. They flutter like leaves. I bite my lip and grab one of the papers before wiping the rest of them away. It says CHRISTOPHER COONLUMBUS, which I think is pretty funny. The first time they tagged my car, I cried with Melanie about it. Now I wipe away the flyers. I get in my car and hit the preset for my place. The car starts moving, and I recline for a nap. I'll be half-asleep when I get home, and I won't have time to think about anything before I'm gone in bed.

I wake up thinking about putting on a tie. When I got the promotion, the first thing I bought was a new tie. I imagine Melanie looking at me, her face soft with admiration. I imagine her nodding and smoothing out my collar. I don't know why I imagine that because she rarely did that kind of thing even when we were together. She definitely never did that kind of thing after that article, "Injustice Park: The Pay-to-Play Death of Morality in America," came out and the protesters started getting national coverage. Every day for a month, the news trucks circled around the park. Then they got bored and left, and it was just the protesters again. They weren't going to get bored. After all that, even at home, I was a sellout for months.

"Why do you still work there, Zay?" she'd say when I was up late drafting a proposal for a new module on my own time with no guarantee anybody would even see the work.

"'Cause it's a solid job," I'd say, even though that wasn't the reason at all.

Then she'd say something like, "What's a job without a soul?" And then I'd stop what I was doing and consider explaining to her for the millionth time that I hadn't sold my soul.

"But it's okay for you to eat here? To live here? That's cool?" I'd say instead. And I wouldn't bother with my usual argument: that it was better for me to get fake blasted ten or twenty million times a day than for an actual kid to get murdered out of the world forever. Did anyone ever think of that, ever?

"Really?" she'd say. Then I'd feel bad for making her feel bad about not having a job. We were a good team, and before Zimmer Land, we rarely made each other feel bad on purpose.

"I'm sorry," I'd say, and go from wherever I was in the apartment to right beside her.

And she'd be, like, "I just don't want you doing things that aren't you." And she'd rub my back, and I'd remember I love her for real and have since sophomore Theatre Players.

After Melanie left me, Saleh asked me if I hated her.

To be funny, I answered like this, "On a scale from one to five, one being 'not at all' and five being 'absolutely and I'd pay money to go back even though she shattered my heart to pieces when she left me and then, when she got with Heland, it was like she took those pieces and somehow further obliterated them to some kind of heartdust that she then sprinkled into the sun,' I love her a five." We laughed at that.

I can imagine Melanie looking at me now as I'm tightening my tie and ready almost an hour before I need to be, heading to the creative meeting I always said I'd get to.

Why do you still work there, Zay?

Well, Melanie, I think as I look in the mirror one last time, *because maybe there's a version of the park that isn't complete trash. And also because, even though it makes me want to rip my eyes out when I see you with Heland, at least I still see you, and sometimes we even speak. That's why.*

I manual-drive all the way there. I park in the employee lot. It's sunny outside, and we won't open until almost two. It's not even nine thirty. Creative meets at ten. I see cars in the lot. It's disappointing. I wanted to be first. I wanted everyone to sit down after I was already seated and for each of them to take note of me.

Most of the lot is roped off with police tape and KEEP OUT signs. Beyond the taped-off space there are plaster walls that hide the new module they're building.

In front of the construction site, there's the trailer that management uses for meetings.

I open the door. The trailer is full. Everyone gets quiet and looks at me the way little kids look at themselves when one of them has done something wrong. Heland's floating head speaks first. "Thanks for joining us, Isaiah," his hologram says, smiling kindly. Heland Zimmer, the CEO of Zimmer Land. In person, he looks like he wakes up every morning and chops a few trees down before eating half a dozen raw eggs. When he's projecting via HoloComm, he's a giant head with a beard.

Also, he's white, a fact protesters remind me of very, very often. Heland is an idiot. An idiot who thinks he's doing the right thing. I think. An idiot with a black girlfriend named Melanie, which probably makes him at least 20 percent less racist in the eyes of consumers according to some focus group somewhere.

"What?" I say. The others on the creative team are looking at me.

"We're just getting ready to wrap up, but have a seat."

I look at Heland's floating head.

"Sorry," I say.

"Don't worry about it, get comfortable," Heland says. Chairs scoot up so I can pass. There aren't any seats left, so I stand in the back of the room next to a table bearing the carcass of a fruit platter and a puddle of coffee. "All right," Heland continues. "As you know, it has been a trying time for us, but we believe our future is secure. Next week, Lot Four will finally open up, and with it, a new chapter in interactive justice engagement. Doug, wanna take it from here?" Doug is sitting down with a laptop in front of him. Doug is Heland's right-hand guy. He's the president of park operations and leads the creative team. Once, after I'd fully engaged the mecha-suit, a patron called me a "fucking ape." He'd screamed, "Go back to Africa." I grabbed him by his head. His feet dangled. I hit him once on his side. I punched him so hard I broke two of his ribs. When Doug wrote me up for it, he told me it was a formality, not to worry about it. Then, two weeks ago, when I first stopped engaging customers with any real aggression, he said, "Make sure your heart's still in it because somebody else might want the job."

"Love to," Doug says. "Zimmer Land values creativity and innovation, always with its mission in mind." He clicks something on the laptop. The Zimmer Land mission statement hovers in the air behind him in hologram blue.

Zimmer Land Mission
1) To create a safe space for adults to explore problem-solving, justice, and judgment.
2) To provide the tools for patrons to learn about themselves in curated heightened situations.
3) To entertain.

"The things Zimmer Land aims to do at its core have not changed. And we've delivered with the situational modules we've provided. Now, thanks to the information gathered from our patrons and the creative team's work, we are officially ready to expand Zimmer Land and generate a significant increase in revenue, all while extending the reach of the park into a greater portion of the market. Our new module will spearhead this transition. This is the future of Zimmer Land." There's an unnecessary flash, then the mission statement reappears.

Zimmer Land Mission
1) To create a safe space to explore problem-solving, justice, and judgment.
2) To provide the tools for patrons to learn about themselves in curated heightened situations.
3) To entertain patrons of all ages.

When I see the difference, my throat dries up.

"Starting a week from today, Zimmer Land will officially be open to patrons of all ages. And Lot Four will be revealed as PS 911." The hologram flashes into a three-dimensional represen-

tation of the building soon to be unveiled outside. It's a small
school. Doug explains the basic premise of the new module.
How it will focus on juvenile decision-making/justice imple-
mentation. And how, with only their eyes, their ears, and their
wits, youths will have to figure out who in the building is the
terrorist planning to plant a bomb in the gym. Doug touches
his laptop some more to take us through the halls and explains
how many choices the module will offer patrons: you might
team up with other patrons to stop the terrorist, or maybe
sneak off and take on the terrorists alone, or maybe you aren't
decisive enough and die in a violent explosion. He says the
revisitability of the module will be greater than any module
we've ever had before. "Any questions?" he finishes.

Somebody asks who the primary players will be. Doug explains there will be some new hires coming in for training this
week and also that any current players who want a shot should
audition the following week. I raise my hand.

"Does this mean the other modules will be open to kids
now?" I know the answer, but I want to see everybody hear it
plain and clear.

"Well, yes," Doug says. "Even our most popular outfits have
started to see a sort of dry spell. The new traffic should allevi-
ate that and create some dynamic new possibilities."

"And, of course, we'll start some testing in this new direction this week before we go live," Heland says.

"Any other questions?" Doug asks. Everybody's quiet because everybody wants to go. I have a lot more questions. "All
right, that's great, guys," Doug says. "I'm really excited to see
what we can do these next few weeks."

Heland's giant head nods. That's the signal for everybody to
go. I watch the others leave. Doug is the only other black person on the creative team. I was going to say something about

that in the meeting—just as a talking point, just as something
to get everyone thinking about what the park is doing and what
it could do.

I don't leave with everyone else. Doug sits down. Heland
blinks.

"I was told the meeting was going to be at ten," I say. I've already pulled up the email from Doug, which clearly said ten.

"Oh, that's my bad," Doug says as I push the screen toward
his face. When I see he's not interested, I take it back. "That
was the old meeting time; I meant to switch that."

"No harm, no foul," Heland says, smiling. "Nine from now
on, sound good?"

"I had some things I wanted to bring up in the meeting." I
have several things I wanted to bring up. "I think Cassidy Lane
needs some big changes."

"Cassidy Lane is still the most profitable of all the modules," Doug says, looking at Heland, not me.

"What's on your mind?" Heland says. I can't not think about
Melanie when I see Heland.

"Well, I think we need to offer more choices in the prep so
the firearm option doesn't seem like the only one that will be"
—I pause looking for the word that I think they'd want to hear
—"entertaining. Right now, I think the module is kind of flat.
It could be a lot more dynamic. There are a lot of opportuni-
ties before the patron-meets-player portion of the module for
some interesting problem-solving work."

"I mean, I hear you, Isaiah," Doug says. "But it sounds like
you want to take the thing that makes the module entertaining
and strip it down. It's about being dunked into a situation and
making the hard choice. How do you have real justice without
life-and-death decisions? You know, some fireworks. You don't.
That's how."

I look at Doug. "I've been working the module for more than a year. The majority of the patrons are revisitors who just want to kill me over and over again. It isn't a hard choice for them. I think we could make killing a less obvious option, and we could also make the killing, if they do choose that, matter more in the postsequence. It'd be more intense. I've drafted a thorough plan for an accessory to Cassidy Lane, which they could pay for in advance, that would take them through a trial process, where maybe they could find out that their decision to kill leads to a life in prison. Or they might have to meet the family of the guy they killed or something."

"I hear you, and you should definitely send me any plans you have," Doug says. "But it's important to remember that we want to capture that visceral, intense, in-your-face moment when justice is begging you to do something and—"

"I think we're equating killing and justice for our patrons," I say flatly.

"Well, sometimes it's the same," Heland says. "And sometimes it isn't. That's the magic of the module."

"Another thing." I know Heland and Doug want to go, but I have a lot more to say. "I don't think the mecha-suit is necessary anymore. It isn't realistic enough to justify itself in the module."

"You're killing me," Doug says. "The moment when you activate your suit is literally the point of all modules, where patrons feel most viscerally connected to the experience. That's the exact feeling we're going for. We need it. Plus, it protects you. It's a liability issue."

"How many teenagers in the world can afford a mecha-suit? It's surprising, but it isn't real life. A kid wouldn't have a mecha-suit. He wouldn't be able to become a tank and fight off a grown man. He wouldn't fight through gunshots." I realize I'm breathing hard, so I try to slow down.

"I get that," Doug says, closing his laptop. "These ideas are all worth exploring, for sure. Send me an email, and we'll rap at the next meeting." Creative meets once a month.

"That's great. I like your enthusiasm, Isaiah," Heland says.

"Thanks," I say, and I walk out of the trailer leaving Doug and Heland to discuss other things and ignore what I've just told them.

The first time I really spoke to Heland was at the new-employee banquet. I'd brought Melanie. Heland had told me about his work on Wall Street, how he gave up all that money to be a social worker in Albany. How he'd helped high-risk kids smooth things out and found permanent housing for former addicts. Zimmer Land was the "next step in the evolving face of social interconnectivity and welfare promotion." He said that to me. And it's not that I believed him, but I didn't think he was lying either. Plus, I needed a job.

I head out to go do nothing until it's time for me to come back to the park and work my shift. It's still early, so my car is clean. No flyers asking me what it's like to sell my soul. It's there, in that open lot with no place to hide, that I see her. Getting out of her own car, going to the park to see Doug and maybe talk about the new hires. She's the new head of human resources at the park.

"How can you work here, Melanie?" I'd asked the second time I saw her in the park. The first time I couldn't say anything at all. "Well, I see it now," she'd said. "I get it. Zimmer Land could really actually help people see the craziness all around them."

But that's not what I meant when I asked. I meant how could

she stand to work so near to me and know we would never be the same.

"Hey," she calls. The sound of her voice makes me wish I were a better person.

"Hey," I say, and we both walk closer. When we're only a foot away from each other, we just stand there.

"How was the big meeting?" Melanie asks. At some point, when we were still living together, I'd suggested Melanie try to see if Heland would hire her. I'd been joking, mostly.

Heland had a "talk" with me when he first started seeing Melanie, which was not long after she started working in the park. I don't know when she'd first interviewed; she'd left me already by then. He'd said, "Melanie. Is that cool?" I'd said, "Don't worry about it." Then, two weeks ago, he called me into his office and said that Melanie had suggested me for a spot on the park's creative development team. When he asked if I wanted it, I snapped out of imagining what strangling him would feel like to say, "I'd love that."

"It was awesome," I say to Melanie. She smiles. I stare at her mouth.

"That's great," she says. She touches my shoulder, which makes me feel amazing, then pathetic.

"Yeah," I say, then I walk to my car and she walks to wherever it is she has to go.

Later that day I have ten walk-throughs. Eight times out of ten, I get murdered.

That night I dream about getting killed. Murdered by a bullet. I dream this dream often. But this time, after I'm dead, I feel my soul peeling from my body. My soul looks down at the body, and says, "I'm here."

People say "sell your soul" like it's easy. But your soul is

yours and it's not for sale. Even if you try, it'll still be there,
waiting for you to remember it.

The next day, before we open, we have a park-wide meeting
with all the players from the different modules gathered in the
area just in front of Lot Four. The new module is up. There's
an American flag flapping on the front lawn of the little school,
and a sign that says PS 911 up front. Melanie is up on a small
platform in front of Lot Four along with Doug and a hologram
of Heland's head. Today Heland's body is meeting with inves-
tors in Cabo.

"You okay?" Saleh pokes my side. Saleh's half-Indian, half-
Irish. She usually plays one of three Muslims who may or may
not have something to do with a terror plot that could lead to
the death of several passengers on a train from city A to city B
in the Terror Train module.

Heland explains first that he's very happy with all the hard
work we've been doing and that we should all know the park
couldn't exist without us. "The face of real-time justice-action
is changing. We were the first, and it's only right that we continue to innovate and provide the world with life-changing ex-
periences that foster real growth." Then Heland announces
that Zimmer Land will now be open to children. He explains
that the newest module, the school behind him, PS 911, will
actually be curated explicitly for youths. Saleh grabs my hand,
then lets it go. Some other players look at one another awkwardly. Melanie bites her lip. At least she knows.

"Now, things will be a little different in terms of the patrons
we see, but your jobs will be essentially the same. Keep pushing for the visceral," Doug says in his heavy, comforting voice.

"If you have any questions about the future of Zimmer

Land, please see me" — Doug points to himself — "and if you're new and you have questions about your position and how to fit your role, please see Melanie."

"Okay, that's all," Heland says. The crowd lingers a little, then floats away.

"Jesus," Saleh says.

"I know," I say.

"We have to get out of here," she says. "At least before it was, like, maybe we could have done some kinda good."

"We still can, maybe," I say to convince myself as much as her. "We can still change some people."

"We have to get outta here," Saleh says.

"I just got put on creative development."

"So what?"

"So I can't just quit."

"You can do whatever you want," Saleh says.

"Don't quit," I say.

"Wow," she says. We look at each other, then she hugs me. Then she's gone. And I go to Cassidy Lane.

In the bathroom of house 327, I get ready. I skim the updated protocol that explicitly says not to touch the kids. All children wear green bracelets. I may, however, engage in the usual measured violence with of-age patrons in front of the children.

I'm walking through the lane. Minding my business or up to no good, just like every other person in the world. Door 336 opens. I see a man walk outside. He stretches on his front lawn, then turns to me. I don't know the man's name, but he's come to shoot me so many times it's almost like we're family. Then I see his son peeking out of the house. A little kid, as promised. He might be eleven. His father stomps in my direction.

"Hey, you're not up to any trouble out here, are you?" the

patron says. He's got a little bit of gut that sags out over his pants. Probably in his early forties. His hair is chopped close to the head. He's wearing a shirt with a knight on it, a local high school team's mascot. He always wears it. It's his killing shirt. It's stained a brownish red already.

"No," I say flatly.

"Well, I think you're out here causing trouble." The kid is out on the lawn now. He has a hat that's a little too big for him on his head. We're only a few mailboxes apart.

"Well, if you think that, what am I supposed to do?"

His face reddens. "Listen, this is where I live, and I'm not going to have you causing trouble in my home."

"Trouble like what?" I ask.

"Listen, either you leave right now or we're gonna have problems."

"You know what?" I yell, and then he hits me in the stomach. I fall to my knees and try to take a breath. I feel the mecha-suit begging me to make this easy. I get up slowly. I put the trigger on the ground.

"Come on, get out of here!" he says. He shoves me down again. I jump up, push his arms away.

"Are you happy now? Are you?" I scream.

"Dad!" His kid comes running to his side.

His young, green-bracelet-wearing hand clings to his father's jeans as the patron pulls the gun from his waist.

"Stay behind me," he says to his kid.

FRIDAY BLACK

Get to your sections!" Angela screams.

Ravenous humans howl. Our gate whines and rattles as they shake and pull, their grubby fingers like worms through the grating. I sit atop a tiny cabin roof made of hard plastic. My legs hang near the windows, and fleeces hang inside of it. I hold my reach, an eight-foot-long metal pole with a small plastic mouth at the end for grabbing hangers off the highest racks. I also use my reach to smack down Friday heads. It's my fourth Black Friday. On my first, a man from Connecticut bit a hole into my tricep. His slobber hot. I left the sales floor for ten minutes so they could patch me up. Now I have a jagged smile on my left arm. A sickle, half circle, my lucky Friday scar. I hear Richard's shoes flopping toward me.

"You ready, big guy?" he asks. I open one eye and look at him. I've never not been ready, so I don't say anything and close my eyes again. "I get it; I get it. Eye of the tiger! I like it," Richard says. I nod slowly. He's nervous. He's a district manager, and this is the Prominent Mall. We're the biggest store in his territory. We're supposed to do a million over the next thirty days. Most of it's on me.

The main gate creaks and groans.

"I saw the SuperShell in the back. What's she wear, medium or large?"

"Large," I say, opening both eyes.

There's a contest: whoever has the most sales gets to take home any coat in the store. When Richard asked me what I was going to do if I won, I told him that *when* I won I was going to give one of the SuperShell parkas to my mother. Richard frowned but said that was honorable. I said that, yeah, it was. The SuperShells are the most expensive coats we have this season: down-filled lofted exterior with a water-repellent finish, zip vents to keep the thing breathable, elastic hem plus faux fur on the hood for a luxurious touch. I know Richard would have me choose literally anything else. That's half of why I chose it. I set it aside in the back. It's the only large we've got due to a shipment glitch. Nobody will touch it because I'm me.

Most of the Friday heads are here for the PoleFace™ stuff. And whose name is lined up with the PoleFace™ section on the daily breakdown each day this weekend? It's not Lance or Michel, that's for sure. It's not the new kid, Duo, either. I look across to denim where Duo is pacing back and forth making sure his piles are neat and folded. He's a pretty good kid. Sometimes he'll actually ask to help with shipments. He wears a T-shirt and skinny jeans like most of our customers his age. Angela tells him to watch me, to learn from me. She says he's my heir apparent. I like him, but he's not like me. He can sound honest, he knows how to see what people want, but he can't do what I can do. Not on Black Friday. But he'll survive denim.

Michel and Lance cover shoes and graphic tees. Michel and Lance might as well be anybody else. Lance is working the broom.

There's a grind and a metallic rumble. Angela is in the front.

She's pushed the button and turned the key. The main gate eats itself up as it rolls into the ceiling.

"Get out of here!" I yell to Richard. He runs to the register where he'll be backup to the backup safe.

Maybe eighty people rush through the gate, clawing and stampeding. Pushing racks and bodies aside. Have you ever seen people run from a fire or gunshots? It's like that, with less fear and more hunger. From my cabin, I see a child, a girl maybe six years old, disappear as the wave of consumer fervor swallows her up. She is sprawled facedown with dirty shoe prints on her pink coat. Lance walks up to the small pink body. He's pulling a pallet jack and holding a huge push broom. He thrusts the broom head into her side and tries to sweep her onto the pallet jack so he can roll her to the section we've designated for bodies. As he touches her, a woman wearing a gray scarf pushes him away and yanks the girl to her feet. I imagine the mother explaining that her tiny daughter isn't dead yet. She pulls the little girl toward me. The girl limps and tries to keep up, and then I have to forget about them.

"Blue! Son! SleekPack!" a man with wild eyes and a bubble vest screams as he grabs my left ankle. White foam drips from his mouth. I use my right foot to stomp his hand, and I feel his fingers crush beneath my boots. He howls, "SleekPack. Son!" while licking his injured hand. I look him in his eyes, deep red around his lids, redder at the corners. I understand him perfectly. What he's saying is this: My son. Loves me most on Christmas. I have him holidays. Me and him. Wants the one thing. Only thing. His mother won't. On me. Need to feel like Father!

Ever since that first time, since the bite, I can speak Black Friday. Or I can understand it, at least. Not fluently, but well enough. I have some of them in me. I hear the people, the sizes, the model, the make, and the reason. Even if all they're doing is foaming at the mouth. I use my reach and pull a medium-size blue SleekPack PoleFace™ from a face-out rack way up on the wall. "Thanks," he growls when I throw the jacket in his face.

I jump down from the cabin and swing the reach around so none of them can get too close. The long rod whistles in the air. Most of the customers can't speak in real words; the Friday Black has already taken most of their minds. Still, so many of them are the same. I grab two medium fleeces without anyone asking for them because I know somebody wants one. They howl and scream: daughter, son, girlfriend, husband, friend, ME, daughter, son. I throw one of the fleeces toward the registers and one toward the back wall. The crowd splits. Near the registers, a woman in her thirties takes off her heel and smashes a child in the jaw with it just before he can grab the fleece. She inspects the tag, sees it's a medium, then throws it down on top of the boy with a heel-size hole in his cheek. I toss two large fleeces and two medium fleeces into the crowds. Then I deal with the customers who can still speak, who are nudging and pushing around me.

"C-C-COAL BUBBLE. SMALL, ME! COAL!" a man says while beating his chest. I'm the only one at work who doesn't have a Coalmeister! How can I be a senior advisor without? The only one!

I press the end of my reach against his neck to keep his hungry mouth from me. Then, without taking my eyes off him, I grab one of the Coalmeister bubble coats from the rack behind me. And then it's in his hands. He hugs the coat and runs to the register.

"Us? US!" the woman with the gray scarf says. She has large

gold earrings hanging off the sides of her head. The pink-coat child is at her shins. The child's face is bruised, but she isn't crying at all.

"Can't. The Stuy!" Gray scarf's husband says. Family time needs forty-two-inch high-def. The BuyStuy deal is only while supplies last! Can't afford any other day.

Black Friday takes everybody differently. It's rough on families. They can't always hear what I hear.

"Asshole!" the wife seethes. Then she stares back at me.

"PoleFace™. Pink," she says, pointing to her child. "Coal SleekPack," she continues, pointing to her own face. A new kiddie PoleFace™, a new coal SleekPack, a Coalmeister. A family set.

The woman has both the coats she needs in a second, then storms off, dragging her child behind her.

It isn't always like this. This is the Black Weekend. Other times, if somebody dies, at least a clean-up crew comes with a tarp. Last year, the Friday Black took 129 people. "Black Friday is a special case; we are still a hub of customer care and interpersonal cohesiveness," mall management said in a mall-wide memo. As if caring about people is something you can turn on and off.

In the first five hours, I do seven thousand plus. No one has ever sold like that before. Soon I'll have a five-hundred-dollar jacket as proof to my mother that I'll love her forever. When I imagine how her face will look as I give it to her, my heart beats faster.

At five in the morning, the lull comes. The first wave of shoppers is home, or sleeping, or dead in various corners of the mall.

Our store has three bodies in the bodies section. The first came an hour in. A woman climbed the denim wall looking

for a second pair her size. She was screaming and rocking the
wooden cubby wall so hard that the whole thing almost fell on
Duo and everybody in his section. Duo poked her off the wall
with his reach. She fell on her neck. Another woman snatched
the SkinnyStretches from her dead hands. Lance came with the
pallet jack, his broom, and some paper towels.

My first break is at 5:30 a.m. On my way to clock out, I walk
through denim.

"Looks like you've had it pretty crazy," I say to Duo. There
are jeans everywhere. None of them folded. Bloodstains all
over the floor.

"Yeah," he says. A young man in a white T-shirt staggers toward us. "Grrrrr," he says. He's gnawing on something. I move
to sling him one of the SlimStraights in his size—he thinks it'll
make him popular at school—but stop because of how quickly
Duo tosses the right kind of jeans to the customer, who takes
them and limps to the register.

"You understand them?" I ask.

"Now I do," Duo says. He kicks at a tooth that's lying on the
ground. Then he shows me a small bloody mark in the space
between his thumb and forefinger.

"That's Black Friday."

"This is my first."

"Well, the worst part is done," I say, kind of smiling, trying
to see where he's at.

"I don't know," he says.

"Yeah," I say, and continue on toward the register.

"My break is after yours," Duo says. That's retail for Hurry
up, I'm hungry.

I punch my username and password into the computer, and
Richard bows down to me like I'm to be worshipped. Angela
nods at me like a proud mama. While I'm gone, Angela will

take my spot in the PoleFace™ section. It's the lull, so she can handle it.

Outside the store, the Prominent is bloody and broken, so I can tell it's been a great Black Friday. There are people strung out over benches and feet poking out of trash bins. Christmas music you can't escape plays from speakers you cannot see. Christmas is God here.

I'm hungry. My family didn't really do the Thanksgiving thing this year—which felt like a relief except I missed my chance for stuffing. I'd offered to help with some of the shopping. My mom had lost her job. I make $8.50 an hour, but I saved. Mom, Dad, sister, me. But then we skipped the whole thing because we don't really like one another anymore. That was one of the side effects of lean living. We used to play games together. Now my parents yell about money, and when they aren't doing that, we are quiet. I walk, wondering if there's stuffing anywhere in the mall.

My second Black Friday, our store was doing pretty well, so there was a commission. You got something like 2.5 percent of all of your sales. It was a big deal for us on the floor. That was when Wendy was sales lead. Which meant she had the highest sales goals. That year she'd brought in a pie for everybody. I made sure not to eat any of it because I don't eat anything anybody tries to shove down my throat, and she couldn't stop talking about the pie. "We can have Thanksgiving in the store! It's homemade." Everybody was saying how nice she was, how thoughtful. Then Wendy and I were the only ones who didn't have the shits all day.

Who knows what she put in the pie. I made it my mission to beat her. And I did. I squashed her. Maybe it was because, thanks to her biological warfare, I had shoes, graphic tees, hats, plus denim to cover while she was stuck in PoleFace™.

Maybe it was because winter was warm that year. Maybe it was that I'm the greatest goddamn salesman this store has ever seen and ever will see. But I squashed her. I've been lead ever since. Wendy was gone by New Year's. I put the extra commission money toward some controllers for my GameBox.

I make it to the food court where the smell of food wafts over the stench of the freshly deceased like a muzzle on a rabid dog. There are survivors, champions of the first wave, pulling bags stretched to their capacity. Using the last of their energy to haul their newly purchased happiness home. And there are the dead, everywhere. I get two dollar-menu burgers, a small fry, and a drink from BurgerLand. The man at the cash register has seen so much and had so much caffeine that I have to remind him to take money from me. Even as he takes it, he stares forward, past me, looking at nothing. I sit at one of the white tables in the food court that doesn't have a corpse on it.

I bite into my burger and chew slowly. If I hold a bite in my mouth long enough, it softens into something that feels almost like stuffing. While I eat, a woman drags a television in a box to the table in front of me. She pushes a woman who is lying facedown in a small puddle of red blood out of the chair. Then she sits down. I recognize her from the store. One of her ears looks like it's been mangled by teeth; the other still has a large gold earring. Her gray scarf is gone. But she's wearing her new coat. When I look at her, she hisses and shows her pointy white teeth.

"It's okay," I say. "I helped you." She looks at me, confused. "Um, SleekPack, coal," I say in Black Friday, pointing to myself, then back to her. The creases on her face smooth. She relaxes into her seat and rubs her cheek into the faux fur of the hood.

"Good haul?" I ask. She nods hard and pets the face of the television box. "Family still shopping?" I ask.

The woman dips her pointer finger into the blood puddle in front of her.

"Forty-two inches, high-def," she says.

This is the only time they can afford it.

With a red finger she makes a small circle, then points two small eyes onto the cardboard box, and drags a smile beneath the eyes. The blood dries out before she gets all the way across the face.

"What?" I ask.

"Dead," she says. "BuyStuy. Trample."

"Oh," I say. "Right."

"She was weak. He was weak. I am strong," the woman says as she pets the face on the box. It hardly smears at all. "Weak," she repeats.

"Got it," I say.

I finish one burger, then I toss the second to the woman. She catches it, tears the paper away, and eats gleefully. My phone moves in my pocket and I grab it. I still have fifteen minutes, but it's the store.

"We need you!" Richard screams.

"I just left," I say, getting up and starting to walk.

"Duo just quit."

"Oh."

"He said he needed to go on break, and I said wait a few minutes, and then he just left. He's gone."

"I'm coming," I say.

I get up, walk toward the escalator. I step to the conveyor and float down. Coming up on the opposite escalator is Duo.

"Hungry?" I say.

"I couldn't do it, man. That shit is sad," Duo says.

I grunt something because I don't have the words to tell him that it is sad but it's all I have.

"It's a nice coat," he says. "But that's it."

"What?"

"The coat isn't proof. She knows. You don't need to, bro," he says, turning around and rising up the escalator.

"Don't do that," I say. "Not to me."

"Sorry."

"Yeah," I say, and then Duo flies away.

My third Black Friday, the company wasn't doing great. There was no commission and no prize. I still outsold everybody.

Back in the store, there's a new body in the body pile and in PoleFace™ a young woman is trying to kill Angela. She's clawing and screaming, and even from the store entrance, I know what she wants. Angela is pinned against the wall where the SuperShells are. It looks like the girl is about to bite Angela's nose off. Lance is rolling a teen toward the body pile, and Michel is helping a customer in the shoe section. Richard looks at me and points to Angela and the girl. I know what the girl wants.

"Help!" Angela yells, turning to look at me. She has a reach between her and the girl, but she won't last much longer. I turn and go to the back room. I look up at the only large SuperShell parka hanging there. I pull it off the hanger. I go outside, and the girl can smell it. She looks in my direction and howls like a wolf.

I won't be alone with this, she's saying. They'll like me now.

She rushes toward me. I dangle the coat out to the side like a matador. She runs toward it, and I let go and leap out of the way as she comes crashing through the parka. Then with the coat in her hands, she says, "Thank you," in a raspy voice.

I watch her at the register. "Have a nice day," Richard says, as he rings her up. She growls, then says, "You, too." I punch back in at the computer. Angela puts a hand on my shoulder. "Thanks," she says.

"Yup," I say, and then I go back to my section.

A herd of shoppers stops in front of the store. They see the PoleFace™ we have left. I climb on top of my cabin. The people stampede. Some bodies fall and get up. Some bodies fall and stay down. They scream and hiss and claw and moan. I grab my reach and watch the blood-messed humans with money in their wallets and the Friday Black in their brains run toward me.

I smile out at the crowd. "How can I help you today?"

They push and point in all directions.

THE LION & THE SPIDER

He yelled and jumped at us, making the long fingers of his left hand Lion's claws that viciously tickled our ribs. "One, two, three rabbit children all swallowed up in one bite," my father roared. We jumped and laughed and screamed. He shook the bed we, the children, shared. But watching way up above us was another character who hid in the fist of his right hand, which opened slowly. Anansi the spider appeared before us. "You silly cat," Anansi said before scurrying to the woods, across the mattress and our heads, his tiny legs quick-moving fingers. He disappeared into the bush searching for something special.

Graduation was two weeks away. My father: gone for months.

The day he'd left, my father had said, "I have some business I need to see to."

"And you're leaving today?" I'd said as evenly as possible. I had become a devotee to a religion of my own creation. Its most integral ritual was maintaining a precise calm especially when angry, when hurt, when terrified. People like my father, who yelled freely in English and Twi whenever things were bad, were heretics to be ignored or hated.

"Yes. Flying out later. I'll be back in two weeks. Your mother is doing fine. The doctors say she's all right. You're in charge for now. Make sure your sister keeps up with her studies." He'd handed me forty dollars. This was the first I'd heard of the trip. He would fly across an ocean to the country where both he and my mother were born and raised.

"Be back soon," he'd said that afternoon as he got into the cab.

"Okay. I'll see you later, I guess."

When he'd first left, I'd gone to my mother. She'd been quiet and reserved. She'd been sick for a long time by then. Unable to work, she spent most of her days in our house. Then foreclosure swept us up, and she spent most of her days in the apartment we'd rented my senior year.

"He'll be back soon," she said. Her calm hurt and impressed me.

Now, after months without, I'd decided that he wasn't coming back and was settling into life at the home improvement store. I spent five to eleven, six days a week, digging away at the guts of dusty, cavernous shipment trucks. My title was "unload specialist." There were three of us.

If our adventures unpacking the truck were made into a movie, Cato, who was only a few years older than I was, would have been the strapping young hero. The one you looked to in times of crisis. The other guy, Reese, was probably the same age as my father. He would be the wily old adventurer on his last legs, on the brink of giving up, a few missed cigarettes from a breakdown, but persisting because his experience in the field made him one of a kind, because he was the only one of us who knew how to use the forklift, and because maybe he hadn't quite found his treasure yet. My role, I knew, was the guy who would lose an arm in the second half of the film, maybe saving one of the other two, or one of the real stars would get hurt saving me, which would set me up to lead in the sequel. We were the Unload Team, not unlike the Justice League or the Avengers. The Specialists.

Before every shift, we tossed on red and blue vests, and were transformed. They were thin nylon, weightless but still annoying. Reese wore a company-issued back supporter. Cato wore one of the company hats turned backward. I didn't have any special thing, but not having a thing when the other two did was kind of like having a thing in its own way.

To start a shift, Carter, the overnight manager, would give us something like a pep talk as our cave of untreasures backed into the receiving bay. *Beep.* "We've got two big ones coming." *Beep.* "But I know we can bust these things down." *Beep.* "All the pallets are out, and there's a forklift ready." *Beep.* "Let's get it." *Beep.* "Let's fucking go!" There was a thunderous cough when the mouths of the goliath white trailers kissed the opening of the bay.

We spent most of our time in that receiving bay: a huge concrete space with three giant garage doors. Reese would bring a bolt cutter to the lock that kept the trailer's door closed. We made a little ceremony of it. Reese's veins would puff from his neck as he squeezed the cutter's arms together. We cheered when the metal snapped. Once the bolt was cut, Cato and I would pull the door and slide it up with a careful push. Sometimes an avalanche of tile sets, or caulking material, or whatever would fall out.

We used wood pallets to group things together. We had a

system. "Have gloves on whenever you're back here," Reese had said early on. We used gloves with red wax on the fingers, but I still pulled splinters out of my palms almost daily.

Lion was very pleased with himself. His belly was full—at that, my father put air in his stomach and rubbed it to remind us what a full belly looked like. "It is a shame, though," Lion said, while rubbing his belly. "I was in such a rush to eat I didn't even get to taste the rabbit children."

Lion fell asleep happily in a tree. In his sleep he dreamed of how shocked Rabbit Mother would be when she saw that her family had disappeared. Lion smiled as he thought of the trickster Anansi, who would have no time to plan some foolishness to keep him from the magic potion he'd promised if Lion was able to beat him in a race to the mountaintop.

For the Specialists, the truck trailers were villain, purpose, and home. Between eight and nine, we'd get to the heavy stuff, the big appliances. We'd use hand trucks and pallet jacks. Sometimes Reese had to drive one of the forklifts up into the truck. A fully preassembled workbench moves about as easily as an elephant, but dryers are lighter than you would expect.

One time Cato went for a tower of two stacked washing machines held together by a web of translucent blue plastic wrapped around the middle of their two cardboard boxes. "Hercules," he called out to us as he slid the lip of his hand truck underneath the cardboard. He kicked it farther in, then pulled back. That was his catch phrase. He'd say "Hercules" when he was showing off, soloing stuff that probably needed more than one person.

"Hercules," I called back in support as I pulled a dryer onto a pallet jack. I was the sidekick and proud of it.

Cato made a sound like a piece of food was caught in his throat. By the time I looked up, the two washing machines were teetering, then tackling down. I made a lunge in his direction, but the crash came first. I yelled. Reese dragged as I pushed the washing machines off Cato. Our fear made us strong, and we tossed the heavy boxes aside quickly but carefully enough not to damage anything, because whenever there were damages to the big machines, the loss-prevention guy tried to chop our heads off.

Cato groaned beneath the boxes. I wasn't sure how he'd be when we got them off him. We moved the washing machines and looked at him. His back on the dusty truck floor, the hand truck above him. "I'm good," he said. The hand truck, as our safety tutorials had explained, had rods on either side that kept you from getting all the way crushed should a load ever be too heavy. He'd been pinned down, bruised up maybe, but he was fine.

"Hercules," he mumbled, laughing off his embarrassment as me and Reese helped him up.

"Hercules," Reese said back.

I didn't have any brothers, but Cato was exactly what I imagined having one would be like. In high school, when Cato was a senior and I was a sophomore, he'd been one of the kinder gods of the school. He had been the second fastest in the state in the two hundred meters, and that meant he didn't really have to be nice to anybody. He'd torn his MCL near the end of his senior year, and it'd been a tragedy for our school. The colleges that had shown interest in him snatched their offers back. And here he was still.

We took our breaks at the same time, and when he had his mother's car, he'd drive me home so I wouldn't have to walk. I'd helped him create a comprehensive list ranking all the women in each of the store's departments based on a complicated at-tractiveness matrix. Later, in response to our list, two cashiers made a list ranking all the guys. Cato, of course, was ranked number one. I'd ranked twelfth, which felt like an accomplish-ment. It was a big department store.

Sometimes, when we had lunch, Cato would get serious, and say something like, "You gotta get outta here, man. Don't get stuck."

I wanted to quit more than I wanted anything else the day Cato got pinned by the washing machines. If I'd known where my father was, if I didn't need every cent of the $10.10 per hour I was making, I would have.

I had to stay. The trucks became night, and dreading the trucks became the day. I went from school to the trucks, and from the trucks to sleep. I hardly saw my sister or my mother. I avoided them. When I did see my sister, I tried to be fatherly. "How was school today?" I'd ask.

"You were there," she'd reply. She was only a few years younger. She did me the mercy of pretending everything was normal. We were good at that. Acting, ignoring our own dis-integrating.

In the foam bed on the floor, I'd whined and tried not to cry. "No! He didn't eat Mother Rabbit's children. It's not fair." I couldn't accept it. The stories my father told us had great power. I made sure to let my outrage sing whenever they veered from the path I believed was best. Not to mention that Mother Rabbit's children happened to have the same names as my sis-ter, my mother, and I did. All his stories found a way to make stars of us.

My father shushed me. "Just listen to the story," he said.

———

My collegiate ascent was a big topic in the shipment bay. The guys cheered me on. They joked that I shouldn't forget them when I was a nuclear physicist or the president or a veterinarian. I didn't tell them that the entire process had been halted by my father's disappearance. If he didn't return, I would remain and work up to a managerial spot. I'd become someone like Carter, a fate that filled me with an anguish that felt like lead in my stomach. So far as they knew, I was deciding between a school upstate, a school in the city, and another one in Connecticut.

"Well, you trust me," Reese said to me one day while I was helping him lay bags of enriched soil out on a pallet. "They're gonna be begging you to fuck 'em wherever you go." Then he smiled the way he did whenever he said something inappropriate, showing his cigarette-stained top teeth.

Reese had long skinny arms, and he always smelled like cigarette smoke. Often, he'd suck on his cheeks and move his mouth like something was stuck to his gums. I didn't know anyone else like him. I would have liked to make him proud, even though, when I'd first started, Cato had put it in my head that Reese was some kind of racist.

"He said something about niggers, man," Cato had told me my third week working in the store. "I heard it, hard *er* at the end of it, too. I'm 98 percent sure. He didn't see me. He was on the phone. I think he was talking to his wife or something."

I didn't like to disagree with Cato if I could avoid it, but I told him that I didn't think Reese was like that. I liked to think that if he was a racist, because of me and Cato, at some point he'd gone home to his wife, and while they were at dinner or just sitting in front of the TV, he'd have something on the tip of his tongue. He'd be fidgety, almost nervous, and eventually he'd say something like, "Did ya know I work with two niggers?" His wife, who was also probably racist, would look up at him, waiting for a point, and after sliding some peas back and forth a few times on his plate, Reese would finish his thought. "They're not so bad." And he'd say it in a way that wouldn't mean that black people were generally okay. That would be too embarrassing for him to admit at almost fifty-two or however old he was. He'd mean it like we, specifically us two, were okay even though somewhere, by extension, he'd feel that maybe he'd been wrong about black people his whole life.

"Ah, Lion, I was beginning to think you had run off into the night," Anansi said the morning of their big race. When he was Anansi, my father's voice was wise and small. "Are you ready to run for the lives of the rabbit family? Remember, you have agreed that if I make it to the top of the highest of the Togo Mountains, you will cut off your own tail and leave the rabbit family alone for good."

Since the night before, Lion's belly had pained him terribly. My father held his stomach and groaned. Lion could feel the three rabbit children in his stomach. They were much heavier than Lion had anticipated.

The middle of the truck always felt endless. There'd be boxes of stuff packed so tightly that they'd cram up against the ceiling. Pulling the wrong thing made the towers fall.

To make things easier, I played little games in my head. Like, I imagined that if we worked fast enough, at the back of the truck, behind that final wall of washing machines and fridges, there would be something amazing: a bag of money, a baby, gold, anything. I'd choose something specific, though. If it was a baby, it'd be a lost child with a name: Cristie. We'd only know this because of the note left behind with her. I'd pull away a Whirlpool, and there she would be, little baby Cristie, a note tucked into the folds of the soft blanket she was wrapped in: *Please take care. I know you are better suited than I am. Please, love her. I love her. I love you, Cristie. Goodbye. I love you.*

The baby and the note would obviously be a shocking discovery even for the Specialists, and for, like, five minutes we wouldn't know what to do. We'd take turns holding the baby, then, almost sadly, we'd call a manager, and he'd call the police. Of course, we'd stop working for the day. For years following, me, Cato, and Reese would all keep track of Cristie; we'd be secret faraway fathers, sending her anonymous little treasures, and she'd be known locally by some kind of nickname that fused baby words and home improvement stuff: Tool-born Tyke. Or whatever.

But when we got to the very end, all that work ended in a tall slab of nothing, always.

"On your mark, set, go!" Monkey called out from a tree. Lion leaped forward toward the base of the mountain to begin his climb. Lion looked back at Anansi, who was already far behind him. When my father became Lion, he made his voice big and mean. "You've grown foolish, spider," Lion said as he began to climb the great mountain. "I am the fastest in the jungle." He thought, *I have already eaten the rabbit children and now I will win this race and you will have to give me your magic potion.* Far behind Lion, Anansi walked through the lands slowly. His head was down, as though he were not interested in the mountain at all.

"Ah, Anansi, why don't you run, oh?" Monkey asked. "Do you not want to save these poor rabbit children?"

"I have already saved the children, brother. Now I will embarrass this silly cat," Anansi said.

"Ah, Anansi. Lion is already at the mountain. If you do not run now, you will surely lose."

"You will see," Anansi said. "You will see."

Years earlier, when we'd had the house, my father had agreed to take my neighbor, Jerry, and me to the movies. We'd looked forward to it all week. My father told us we'd be leaving at 7 p.m. to catch the 7:30 show. The day of, my father's car pulled into the driveway around 6:55. Jerry and I were in the middle of a third round of mashing our controllers. A Japanese martial artist kicked a mutant in the face. "Your father's outside," my mother called. His horn honked once, a long hard blow that almost carried my father's voice on it. I felt him sitting in the car, waiting. We stopped the game and hurtled down the stairs. When we got outside, the slivers of green grass poking through the breaks in the driveway looked homeless compared to the fullness of the lawn.

Jerry looked at me, confused. "He forgot us?" I walked up to the mailbox. My father's taillights were still climbing away up our street. I started waving my arms wildly, running hard up the hill. I wanted it to seem like a joke. Jerry ran with me. I was screaming, "Dad, Dad! We're here! We're here!" Jerry screamed, "Hey! Hey!" The whole time we scrambled, our arms waving like the blow-up thing outside the Nissan dealership. "Dad, Dad!" I called. He slowed down for oncoming traffic, then turned and sped off onto Route 42.

We walked back sweaty and dazed. The fun of our game chasing the car was lost. Jerry said that maybe it was a joke and that we should wait for him to turn around. I said, "Maybe."

We looked to my mother for answers. She poured juice. She watched us drink quietly. After he drank his, Jerry went home. When Jerry was gone, I said, "Why would he just leave us? It was a minute."

"It is just a movie. It will be there," she said.

"But why did he leave us? We were right there."

"Be patient with him. He is not patient. So you must be patient," she said.

"It isn't fair," I said, slowly explaining facts.

"It will be there. He wants to do things his way. He'll take you later," she said.

I was disappointed because I thought it was obvious that I'd never want to go with him anywhere ever again.

"Mother Earth, Mother Earth," Anansi called out. "Mother Earth." The earth shook, as did the foam mattress when my father pulled and pushed it quickly.

"Anansi, you have called my name," Mother Earth called back to Anansi, her voice in the wind and the trees.

"Beautiful Mother Earth, I have a small request to make of you."

"You ask before you give, Anansi?" The earth trembled. Monkey fell out of his tree.

"No! Never! Great Mother, I give in promises and work before I ask," Anansi spoke, and bowed his head to the ground.

"What have you given?" Mother Earth asked.

"I've planted these seeds to you and promise they will add to your beauty," Anansi said without bringing his gaze up from the ground.

"I've seen the work you have done. What is it that you request?"

"I ask only for a small breeze, a kind wind down this path and up the great mountain," Anansi said.

"My son's getting ready to graduate, too," Reese said to me one day in the truck. I grabbed two boxes of beware-of-the-dog and stay-off-the-grass signs.

"What's his name?" I asked.

"He's a junior. Reese Junior. We call him RJ."

"Cool," I said. "Where's he thinking of going?" I had never heard of Reese's son before.

"Probably he'll do a year or two at the community college, then we'll see from there," Reese said.

"I might do that, too," I said. Most people I knew had already committed to glimmering universities. I'd told the school upstate, the school in Connecticut, and the school in the city I'd see them in the fall and that they should expect my initial deposit soon.

"Nah, you won't," Reese said. He was encouraging me. He was sure of my future in a way I was not.

With a small blade of grass in his hands, Anansi felt the great push of Mother Earth. Her hand carried him down the path and up the great mountain. Lion struggled only a few feet from the bottom. Anansi screamed from the top of the winds. "You've got rocks in your belly, you silly cat. I knew you would do evil so I put rocks in the rabbit children's bed." Lion roared and tried to swipe Anansi as he rode his blade of grass up the great mountain. He could not. On the mountaintop, Anansi laughed and laughed.

He reappeared a week before graduation. Three and a half months later than expected. Three months without any contact at all. I was with Reese. That day there was no truck, so they put us in the paint section to support. I saw him before he saw me. I hoped I looked as different as I felt. I felt strong. He noticed me. I felt headless. He waved wildly. He started walking faster, as if he'd just then realized he was late. He wore his jean shorts and his leather sandals. He called my name twice even though it was clear I'd already seen him. He reached me. He put a hand on my shoulder.

"Dad," I said. I thought, *There's food in the fridge because of me. I went to prom. I imagined you gone forever, and I survived.*

I thought, *Thank you.* I don't know why.

Reese looked up from the cans he was arranging. "Is this your dad here?" he said, taking off a glove and offering his hand. "You've got a fine son." My father took it and said in a friendly laugh, "Yes, he's a big man." He turned his attention to me. Reese walked away from us to the other side of the long aisle near different shades of tan and green. "I just got in. Is this your job, waiting around with paint?" He laughed. "I don't want to keep you from your working."

He patted me on the shoulder again.

"Dad," I said, not wanting to be calm but not knowing how to do anything but breathe.

"I'll be waiting in the lot. You need a ride, right?"

I said, "Yes, I do."

LIGHT SPITTER

He wants them to know they made him this way. So he twists a thumb of red from the tube and draws a large *F* on his forehead. It takes him too long to realize he's placed it backward. "Dang it," he says to himself. But he doesn't wash it away and start over. He's past the point of mistakes. He doesn't make mistakes anymore. They were wrong about him. They were for so many years. They were. He sees that clearly now. He is not, has never been, and he never will be wrong. He completes his title, being careful to draw the red onto his head in bold letters they won't be able to forget. The name they gave him, Fuckton, in lipstick. Even with a backward *F* it's glorious. He grabs his gear, then heads out to find his destiny.

Safe in her home, Melanie Hayes says, "Love you, sweetie. Keep at it, all right? We want a better semester, right?" She can imagine her daughter's eyes rolling but figures the nudge is worth it. She's a good student, her daughter, but she's human, and sometimes she gets distracted. They both get distracted, but they've always been a good team. The two of them, now that her husband had opted out of their lives, would have to be especially good together. "Love you," she says again to her college girl. That's what she wants to leave on. It's still early in the semester. She smiles to herself as she listens to her daughter's voice, which sounds annoyed but also soft in that way Deirdra is.

Fuckton grabs Bluntnose, his green comb, and slides a pale finger across its teeth. His hands tremble. He closes his eyes so he can properly appreciate the small *plink* of the teeth bending, then snapping back into place. He brings the comb to his head. Yes. Each strand of hair will shine, slick and erect. The mane of a battle-ready soldier. Oh, he will look good for the annihilation. For this momentous occasion, he is even wearing his contacts. Contacts that almost beefed the whole morning because he'd brushed his teeth before donning them, getting some paste on his fingers, causing his left eye to feel aflame for several minutes. But no matter. Minor mishap. The apocalypse wanes naught to Colgate. A red eye is of little consequence. How many more red eyes? How many great tears will they weep? Ten, twenty, hundreds for each of his. Fuckton pulls Bluntnose through his hair once more. It kisses his scalp so gently. How he will shine on this day of bright retribution.

He lives on the campus and still, no friends. He tried the ensemble-choir mixer. Still no friends. He tried chess club, had handily vanquished the club treasurer. Still no friends. He tried to charm the Campus Democrats at a canvassing meeting and watched a gaggle of liberals as they giggled and guffawed and very clearly texted one another about him. Calling him a dotard of some kind, no doubt, after he'd summoned a tremendous courage and got up and said his piece on the merits of conservative fiscal attitudes. When he'd ventured to the Campus Republicans during their Free to Hate rally, he had been

promptly squirted with the water guns they'd had for some
reason because, apparently, they'd gotten wind that he'd been
consorting with the Democrats and thought him a spy of some
kind. Either way. No friends, some enemies even. But it's always been like this. His whole life. And yet that's what makes
what's to come so much easier. He walks into the warm day
feeling as a giant might before it crushes peasants underfoot.
At the library door he watches a young woman walk out. She
pauses, holds the door for a moment, and when Fuckton stares
at her, smiling, she looks at him in a bored, searching way.
"Hi," Fuckton says. She says nothing in response. Crinkles on
her nose show that she's annoyed he's even tried to speak to
her. The insolence is welcomed. Fuckton walks in giddy with
the power in his hands, the plain-sight secret of it. How, on the
other side of the next few moments, he will be everything he's
always deserved.

From across the library's first floor, Fuckton sees a girl holding her place in a closed book with her thumb. She has a phone
to her ear. Hair wrapped neatly in a scarf. Smiling. She's the
one.

"Easy, lady. I just got here. Don't worry," she whispers, then
hangs up. She needs to focus. It's the first week of her junior
year at Ridgemore University, and she's in the library.

She's there because this year she's finally being honest with
herself: she doesn't get any reading done in bed. Ten, maybe
twenty pages, and she knocks out. Sleep. Then she'll wake up
two hours later and be disappointed in herself and hungry (a
dangerous combination as the first seems to enhance the second), and there are still people who say things like, "Wow, Deirdra! You look so good. I hardly recognized you!" even though

all the weight she'd lost recently was weight she'd gained freshman year, so it never really feels like a compliment exactly.

But last semester, after falling asleep in bed, instead of getting back to the book when she'd wake up, she'd call up Terry and the two of them would go to the dining hall to eat and chat, which would mostly be Terry explaining his boy trouble as she gave him advice he'd later regret ignoring. She's good for that. Advice. She doesn't mind listening. She's straightforward, even blunt. People appreciate it in the long run. After eating her dining-hall salad, she'd be tired again and cuddle into her bed to watch something simple and funny on her laptop, or if she was lucky, she'd feel guilty for the second dinner and head to the gym. Either way, she wouldn't go back to reading, which she needed to do if she was going to get an A in her contemporary lit class and all but guarantee a spot on the dean's list: a nice gift to her mother, who desperately needed and deserved something nice considering what happened with Dad and how badly Deirdra did last semester.

A voice she doesn't know says something; she is half-annoyed and half-relieved when she is yet again forced to look up from her book. Deirdra just barely lets out an "Oh," and then she is dead.

There's a shriek, and Fuckton looks around and sees people sprinting away from him. "S-sorry," Fuckton says before he can stop himself. A ridiculous thing to say, he knows. He stares at the dead girl, the one he himself, with the help of a gray/black pistol nicknamed Whiptail, just banished from the earth. He waits for the glory to fill him. Eyes wide, he absorbs the body in front of him more intimately. The face is so broken. It terrifies him. There's blood everywhere. On his lips, in his hair. He

looks at her one more time, then Fuckton turns and runs. He
trips on a rug edge and falls on his knees. Whiptail blasts a shot
off into the floor. The boom scares Fuckton just as much as it
scares all the running, screaming people. So much running and
screaming. Fuckton gets up and sprints into the bathroom. Inside, there's a boy washing his hands. "Uh," Fuckton says, and
points Whiptail at the boy. The boy turns, then flinches and
crumples to the tile floor as if someone just ripped his spine
from his body. He's pleading. Fuckton pardons the boy by going into the stall without blowing his head off like he did to the
girl outside. That really happened. Fuckton's body is shaking.
He wants to disappear. From inside the stall, which Fuckton
promptly locks shut, he hears the boy get up and run out of
the bathroom. Fuckton grabs Bluntnose from his pocket and
tries to slide the comb through his hair. "Dang, dang, dang!"
Fuckton screams. He wipes his forehead and barely registers
that a red waxy residue sticks to his fingers. His hands won't
stop shaking.

Above him, an angel wrought from the soul of Deirdra
Hayes watches him closely. There is another bang. Fuckton,
the killer, drops in the bathroom stall. The angel smiles, and
two black horns scrape out of her head, and then she leaves the
bathroom.

The ghost of Fuckton walks from the bathroom, drawn to the
angel floating over her former body, which is limp and bent
over the back of a cushy chair. Deirdra and Fuckton see each
other.

"What happened?" Fuckton asks.

Deirdra turns her head and tries to spit on Fuckton, but all
that comes from her mouth are slim rays of light. After trying
and failing to do anything but shine, she says, "You killed her

—me. You killed me." Fuckton stares at the angel. She looks just like the dead girl on the chair used to. Then he looks at the body.

"Oh, yeah. That feels like it was ages ago. My bad," Fuckton says.

"I'm still bleeding," Deirdra says, pointing to the rush pouring from her body's face. People have cleared out around them, and though Deirdra and Fuckton are there in the library, they both know and feel they've been untethered from time and any particular space.

"What about me?" Fuckton asks.

"You shot yourself."

"Did people see it?"

"Nah, but I did. It was the first thing I saw like this." Deirdra gestures toward herself and her new wings. "I could have helped you, but I didn't. I watched you do it. I let you."

Deirdra's wings are small and shiny. They flap slowly, gathering and stretching like a jellyfish. The horns on her head are long, black, and sharp. "So what now?" Fuckton asks.

"I'm an angel now."

"What am I?"

"I think you're kind of nothing," Deirdra says. "You don't get to be anything special."

"Nothing?" asks Fuckton.

"Yeah. Nothing. Look," Deirdra says. She points to Fuckton's chest, where an empty space the size of a fist pulses in his ghost body.

"Whoa," Fuckton says. He puts a hand in his chest and touches the rim of the empty space. "Kinda like Iron Man."

"No. Not like Iron Man. That means pretty soon you'll be nothing."

"How come you know everything?" Fuckton asks.

"When you get like this, it comes with some info. It's flowing into me still."

"Oh."

"I guess it's supposed to be fair, or something. I can fly now. I have wings and stuff, see. You have a nothing, 'cause you're nothing."

"Dang," he says. "Maybe I can fly, too, though." Fuckton jumps in the air. He kicks his legs back, and points his palms to the ground, but falls back to the tiled floor. He lands in the newly formed puddle of Deirdra's blood. He does not disturb the puddle, which grows and grows.

"Nope," he says.

"Sucks," Deirdra says, rolling her eyes.

"Okay, so now what?"

"Why are you asking me? I hate you. You just ruined my everything."

"Are angels allowed to hate?" asks Fuckton.

"I guess so, since if I could, I'd bring you back to life just to watch you die over and over."

"Okay." Fuckton points to Deirdra's head. "Angels have horns?"

Deirdra frowns and brings one of her hands to the horns on her head. She touches one of the horns for a moment, then quickly drops her hand away, as if they burn to touch. "It's a style," she says. "I had a family, you know. Dreams, too."

"So did I," says Fuckton.

"Well." Deirdra shrugs.

"It sure feels like that was a long time ago," says Fuckton.

"It wasn't. You're not even all the way dead yet."

"I'm not?"

"Nah," Deirdra says. "For now, you're a cipher. A corrupted one. Like a ghost but not all the way, I think."

"You don't know the rules yet?"

"No, not everything. Not yet. It's coming to me slowly. Like downloading. But it doesn't matter; you'll be gone soon and I don't know what will happen to you next, but I hope it's bad."

"Dang, I beefed it." Fuckton reaches into his pocket for his trusty Bluntnose. He finds nothing, then he runs his hand through his greasy hair. It isn't greasy anymore. There is nothing on his forehead.

"Yeah, you did," Deirdra says. "I have to go now."

Fuckton looks around. "What about me?"

"Don't you get it? I don't know. I don't care. You're nothing."

"Why do you have to go?"

"I have stuff to do. I can feel it."

"Can I come with you?" Fuckton asks while staring at the body.

"I never want to see you again."

"Please."

"No."

"Please."

"I'm hoping you die," Deirdra says, her body beginning to glow.

"Wait!" Fuckton reaches out to grab at her. There's a flash and a shift.

Deirdra and Fuckton are in a living room with a green carpet and a brown couch with singe marks on the arms. On the television screen there's a helicopter view of Ridgemore University. Fuckton is drawn to the television. A news anchor appears on the screen, and says, "More on the Ridgemore shooting. The shooter has been identified as freshman William Cropper, who is believed to be in custody and in critical condition. Early re-

ports describe him as, quote, 'an off-putting loner.' Right now
there is one confirmed casualty." The newscaster shakes her
head. Then she tosses to Vince Vice, sports anchor. "That's
just terrible, terrible," he says. "On a lighter note, the Twit-
tawa Typhoons absolutely thrashed the Kiliam Hound Dogs in
last night's season opener."

"What? That's it?" Fuckton says. He turns to look at Deirdra, then at the television, then back at Deirdra.

"How are you here?" asks Deirdra.

"I guess I can follow you." Fuckton opens his fist to show
Deirdra that he is holding one of her feathers. It glows in his
hand.

"I'm trying to be nice because I'm transcending, but I really
don't fuck with you. Get it? So give me that." Deirdra floats
down to take the feather away from him.

"I'll give it back later. And transcending?" Fuckton tightens
his fist around the feather and turns his back to the angel.

"Just die already!" Deirdra says, the tips of her horns ignit-
ing into fire. She takes a few careful, calm breaths. The flames
shrink, then whisper to smoke. "Transcending is like a tryout.
I'm trying out for a job—no, a position? I guess, like a station?
I had a choice, and I chose to stay and help."

"I'd like to stay and help," Fuckton says, standing up, keeping his eyes down.

"I don't think you get the same choices," Deirdra says.

"But you aren't sure?"

"No."

"But I can stay for now?" Fuckton looks at her as his hand
moves behind his body. Deirdra can see him pinching his upper
left arm with his right hand through the hole in his chest.

"Whatever," Deirdra says.

"Thanks, I don't know where else to go," says Fuckton. Deirdra stares at him, and as she does, the front door opens. In comes a boy who is just then returning from Wetmoss High School. His name is Porter Lanks. Fuckton immediately recognizes the boy as a fellow member of the bleak-black-by-yourself. Porter's thin body and slight hunchback make him look like a question mark. No matter how he moves or stands, you can't help but notice the pinkness of his elbows, the dirtiness of his sneakers, the blotchiness of his face. His eyes are wide and blue. Porter's mother is home. "Hi, honey. School okay today?" she asks. She is cooking something, but she stops to look closely at her son as he enters the home.

"It was fine, Mom," Porter says, meeting her eyes just enough. His voice is low and heavy. Mismatched to his body. Porter runs up the stairs into his room. Deirdra follows Porter, and Fuckton follows Deirdra. Porter closes his door, then locks it with a gentle hand. Deirdra and Fuckton slide through the painted wood. Porter takes a pillow from his bed, brings it to his face, and screams into it. Deirdra and Fuckton watch. Fuckton from the ground, Deirdra near the ceiling fan. Porter screams until the sides of his face shade blue. Then, while maintaining a kind of messy silence, he makes as if to tear the pillow in half. He cannot, so instead he straddles it on the bed and punches it several times. His fists fly awkwardly, chaotically.

In a flash the angel and Fuckton are back at Ridgemore University in the bathroom above Fuckton's body, which is limp and pale in the fluorescent light. There's smeared lipstick on his forehead, a hole in his cheek, a gun in his motionless hand. Bluntnose is in the toilet. Paramedics and police surround him.

Loose wisps of toilet paper drink the blood on the floor. A man, a woman, and another man look over the body. One of the medics says, "Maybe he should die."

"Dang," Fuckton says, clawing at his scalp with his fingers.

"You brought us back?" Deirdra asks. "I told you, I have work to do. This doesn't concern me anymore."

"Why aren't they helping?"

"It's 'cause they know what you are." Deirdra looks at Fuckton, and her horns begin to smolder.

"I feel like I could almost . . . " Fuckton reaches out to touch one of the medics, and as he does, he disappears into the man's mind. He sees the man's life. He is a saver of the hurt. He's seen so much brutality. Every day is brutal. Once he saved a man who later killed himself and his entire family. He is repulsed by Fuckton. But still he is a saver of life.

A moment passes, then Fuckton reappears. "I was in his head!" Fuckton says. "I was in his head. I think. Maybe I almost made him help me."

"Nobody wants to help you," Deirdra says. "You don't deserve it. And you didn't do anything but make yourself into more nothing." Deirdra points to the hole in Fuckton's chest that is now the size of a watermelon. She laughs. Her horns erupt into flame again. She stops laughing and closes her eyes.

There's a burst of light.

Back in Porter's room, Deirdra's horns glow like hot steel, then slowly cool to black. "Dang," Fuckton says. He sits cross-legged on a rug. He traces small circles in the ground using Deirdra's feather. Deirdra floats back and forth above. Porter is on the computer, muttering to himself. "I guess a lot of people are pretty scared," Fuckton says.

"Of course. Somebody killed somebody," Deirdra says.

"You mean I killed you." Deirdra stares at Fuckton as he continues. "People called me Fuckton for a long time. Fuckton the blimp, Fuckton the hippo, Fuckton the fuckton. Every day for a long time."

"So?"

"I'm just saying, I'm remembering some stuff. Even after I lost the weight. My name's Billy, but I remember Fuckton more than I remember anything else."

"Sometimes I got bullied, too. I figured it out, though," Deirdra says. "I think, being this way, I'm forgetting some of it. I can't remember everything. But I know I never killed anybody. And I know I hate you."

"Yeah," Fuckton says.

"Yup."

"I guess you didn't really have anything to do with it. It would have been better to get someone I actually knew."

Porter slams his fist on the top of his desk.

"They noticed him today," Fuckton says quietly.

"Who?"

"Them. Everybody. He hates them. They never ever give him one single freaking break." Deirdra floats down and looks past Porter to the computer screen. "He's reading about you now," she says. There's a long block of transcribed text on the computer screen. Fuckton's picture is at the top with a caption that says, *William Cropper, eighteen.*

Fuckton moves to see it. After a few seconds of reading along with Porter, he turns away from the screen. "Yeah, it's me. I guess I'm, like, really famous."

"Not really. But whatever. I'm gonna do my job. I'm gonna help him to not be like you."

"You can do that?"

"I'm gonna try."

"Okay. What should I do?"

"It doesn't matter. I don't care."

Fuckton looks down at the carpet. He slides his hand through his hair.

Deirdra closes her eyes and reaches out. Then she disappears into Porter. Fuckton paces back and forth. He touches the feather in his hand to the rim of the massive hole in his chest. Then he lies down on Porter's bed, clutching the feather. He closes his eyes. When he does, he sees himself crying. That, he remembers, was truly a long time ago. The day he got his gun, Fuckton stopped crying. Instead of crying, he put names on a list and imagined.

Porter cries no tears.

"Are you gonna martyr like me?" Fuckton asks while looking at Porter. "Are you gonna do it?" Porter stares at the screen. Then he crashes his fist onto the desk again. Deirdra tumbles back from nowhere onto the floor.

"Dammit," Deirdra says. Her horns glow hot, and her wings flap erratically.

"What happened?"

"I might have made it worse." Her wings move faster, fluttering behind her. "I pushed up good things. I showed him how happy he used to be. How happy other people are."

"Why would you do that?" Fuckton asks. Porter gets up from the desk and goes into the closet. He digs precisely through some things and pulls out a black handgun.

"A Sig," Fuckton says.

"No! I thought reminding him might help."

"That makes it worse. You're not super good at this."

Deirdra stares at Fuckton. "I didn't know."

Porter looks at the gun in his hands. He cradles it in his

palms. Then he grips it and points it at Fuckton, the wall be-hind him, then at his computer. A warm smile pulls his lips apart. "The Order of the Stingray. Guardians of a great truth," Porter says to himself.

"That's one of my lines, from my note," Fuckton says, jump-ing up. He moves close to Porter. "It's a call for the people like us. To remind the rest of the world that people like us deserve to have what they have. We deserve to have more."

"Okay. I'm sorry your life was that way. But be quiet now," Deirdra says.

"I'm saying I understand him. I used to kind of have this imaginary friend." Fuckton squints as though he is trying to concentrate.

"What?"

"I had this imaginary friend, and he was, like, messed up. More messed up than I was. He had no arms, and he also had, like, Tourette's, so he said random things like 'butt cheeks' or 'lasagna' a lot."

"I don't—"

"He was really nice to me, and he'd try to wave at me, and say, 'Hi,' and I'd say, 'You stupid bitch, you don't even got any arms, get outta here.' But he'd always hang around even though I was only ever mean to him. His name was Lucas. I liked him. I taught him about Stingrays. I know a lot about them. He helped me feel better, I guess. Having someone lower than I was. Somebody who would never leave."

"You're—" Deirdra shakes her head.

"I'd say, 'Hey, catch,' and an imaginary ball would hit him in the face, and he'd say, 'Fuck, cunt, buttersquash,' and I'd say, 'Stingrays are basically sleeker sharks with venom.' And he'd say, 'Almonds!' Or I'd be up in a tree and tell him to come join me. But he couldn't 'cause he had no arms and all. Basically, he'd just smash his face into the bark over and over. It was funny."

"So I should be mean?" asks Deirdra.

There's a knock on Porter's door. Porter freezes. "Ports," his mother says. Porter steps to the door, holding the gun in his hands.

"No!" Deirdra says. Her wings dance and shake. She moves in the air like a bat. The room is silent except for Porter's low breathing.

Porter points the gun toward his mother's voice. "Ports, are you hungry? I can make something quick before dinner. Want a cucumber sandwich?" The pistol's dark mouth hovers inches from the white door. Deirdra floats through the door to look at Porter's mother, then returns. She spins around looking for something to do. Fuckton looks up at her, then at Porter.

"Calm down. Can you help him?" Fuckton says.

Deirdra looks at Fuckton and shakes her head and breathes. For the second time she disappears into Porter's mind. Fuckton waits, watching without moving at all.

"Hey, Ports," the mother says, knocking hard with the knuckle of her middle finger.

"I'm all right, Mom," Porter says while leaning his cheek against the door.

"All right, I'll be downstairs," she says. Porter moves away from the door. Deirdra reappears, smiling.

"Yes," she says with a shimmy of her shoulders. A ring of light floats above her horns. Deirdra reaches up to the left horn, which is now ivory, and tugs down at it. She pulls the horn until it snaps off her head. It turns to sand in her hands and floats to the floor. She tries to grab the other horn, but it hisses with heat when she touches it. Fuckton looks up at her. An angel with a black horn and a new halo. "It means I'm more legit now," Deirdra says, pointing up proudly.

"Oh, all right. Good." Fuckton smiles. Deirdra smiles back, then frowns at herself.

"What's he doing now?" Fuckton asks.

Porter points the gun at a few more invisible people. Then he wraps the gun up in a T-shirt. He puts the gun and shirt in his book bag and zips it up. "No, no, no!" Deirdra says.

"He wants them," Fuckton says. "They deserve to feel bad just once. He feels bad every day. They deserve one bad thing!"

"You don't know anything," Deirdra says.

"I do," Fuckton says quietly. He looks up at the angel. "You did it, though. With his mom. How'd you do that?"

"I showed him something he was forgetting. I used to have a mother," Deirdra says.

The two of them shift through light and time.

They're in a room with hardwood floors. There are posters with athletes and news clippings pinned to the walls. A middle-aged woman is thrashing and crying in a small bed covered in a thick purple comforter. Deirdra looks at the woman, and her black horn explodes entirely into blue flame as she floats down to the bed. Fuckton steps back to a far corner of the room. There's a prescription bottle in the woman's clenched fist.

"Hey, lady, hey," Deirdra says at the woman's side. "It's going to be okay."

"Why's she—"

"You don't speak," Deirdra roars, God in her voice. "She lost her daughter. That's why."

Fuckton touches his hair, then his hole. The woman on the

bed sits upright, then pulls a pillow from the bed and brings it to her face. She breathes deeply into the pillow, then opens up the bottle and pours a mountain of pills into her palm.

"Uh-oh," says Fuckton.

"Hey. Easy. Mom, you're going to be okay." Deirdra cries along with the woman in the bed. "Easy, easy," she whispers.

"Help her. Please," Fuckton shouts.

"I know. I will. I am," says Deirdra, then she disappears into her mother. Deirdra reminds her that in life her daughter was a perpetual force, one that needed to be remembered, loved, even now. That her daughter would never forgive her for ending things this way, and with all the focus she can muster, Deirdra shows her mother her self: her life as this woman's daughter and her new angel life in the background. Before Deirdra even reappears in the room, her mother throws the handful of pills to the floor. They sound like falling hail when they scatter across the floor. Then Deirdra returns and looks at her mother once more.

"You did it," Fuckton says.

"I helped. That was light work. She's strong. I have more to do, but she's gonna be fine."

With another shift, they leave Deirdra's room.

They are with Porter. It is the morning of the next day. Porter looks as if he hasn't slept. While staring into a mirror on his wall, he says, "I am Godlike wrath. I am the Law. Today will be a good day." He leaves his room. He kisses his mother, then hugs her. She receives his hug warmly. Porter goes to wait for his bus. Deirdra and Fuckton follow.

"This one is different. I can't help him. I don't know how," Deirdra says.

"Show him bad stuff. He's like me. Try to show him something like Lucas. Show him maybe it could be worse." The bus comes. Fuckton sits in the first row in the empty seat next to Porter. Porter smiles at each student who passes him as they board.

"Fucking tweak," a tall girl says as she passes. Porter grins greedily at her.

"Sheesh," Deirdra says, looking at Porter. "He doesn't even care anymore."

"Show him bad."

"Will that help?"

"I think it could," Fuckton says, biting his lip.

"Okay." Then Deirdra disappears into Porter's mind.

"I used to hate when they noticed me. I get it," says Fuckton while looking at Porter. "Then you think, if they'd just leave me alone, it'd get better. But then when they leave you alone, they leave you all the way alone. It's just as bad. Worse. It's like you're nothing. Nobody. I hated that. I waited until I got to college. One more chance. I gave them one more chance to fix it, but still nothing. Not one friend. No girls looked at me. No one even tried. And I—I gave them so many chances. Order of the Stingray. I've touched one before. A real stingray. They'd debarbed it, so it wouldn't kill everyone. I felt bad for it. But it's not a real thing. The order isn't real. We aren't wizards. I know you think they deserve it. What do you deserve, though? You think you're already dead. But you're not."

"He can't hear you. And they don't deserve anything! You killed Deirdra Hayes, and look at you now," Deirdra says as she appears back above the two boys. Her wings swing hard and fast. Her voice feels like it's coming from every direction.

"It's just that I know the feeling," Fuckton says, looking down. "I'm remembering more. I'm trying to do what you are. I wanna help."

"*Now* you want to help people."

"I needed help before." Fuckton runs his hand through his hair twice. Then he speaks again. "Did it work?"

"No, it didn't. It wasn't a good idea."

"Dang, okay."

"Yeah," Deirdra says.

"Well, I was thinking, anyway. I probably used you because you seemed like a good person. You looked nice. Like people would care about you. The news and stuff. I remember feeling like that."

"Is that an apology? Never mind. I'm an angel now. Those of my station look forward, not backward."

"Okay, but you said Deirdra; that was your name?"

"Deirdra was *her* name."

"Right."

Porter stands up and walks off the bus. The students swarm toward the school's doors. They laugh and joke as they walk and shove all around him. His fingers strangle his backpack's straps.

"I'm going to remind him that it can be better. I have to try it again."

"Don't do that," Fuckton says as children walk through him. "People will die if you do that."

"People are about to die anyway. It's going to be soon. I have to try."

Fuckton looks up at the angel. "I think, maybe—I think if he knew what I know. Can you show him that?"

"What?"

"That he won't be the great culling, or the changeover, or the beginning of a new era, or whatever. That he'll just be dead in a bathroom. That the Order of the Stingray isn't a real thing. And it won't feel like he thinks. It won't feel good."

"I don't know if I can show him all that. I don't know what killing is like."

"I can show him, maybe. I'll do what you do but with what I know. With this feeling I have. Will you let me?"

Deirdra looks at Fuckton, and then at Porter, who is at his locker, twisting a dial. "I think that all you are is that feeling now. I think that if you give it to him, show it to him, you'll really be nothing," she says, pointing to the hole in his chest.

"Do you think I was always a bad person?" Fuckton asks.

"I don't know. We don't have a lot of time."

"This is the most anyone has ever really talked to me. You know me more than anyone already. Do you think I was always like that?"

"I don't know, probably not," Deirdra says as she floats down to the floor. "I know you've been through a lot. But we don't have time."

"I know." Fuckton opens a hand, releasing Deirdra's feather. It glows and rides the air before settling into her wing. "I wish it was different. I'm sorry. I wasn't always like that."

"I think I can help you show him," Deirdra says. "You probably won't last through it. Okay?"

Porter opens his locker. He puts the bag in his locker and unzips it.

"Let me do it. Before though, do you still hate me?"

"I'm an angel now," she says as she takes Fuckton's hand.

Then the two of them are living through Porter Lanks. They see the halls of Wetmoss High covered in photos of his awkward, naked body. They see Porter standing up to a taller, stronger boy. They feel a fist on their ribs, their nose shattering.

And then they are Porter. They feel him as he pulls a trigger. They are Porter as he watches the people running from him. They watch as he sees himself being the only thing anyone can think or talk about for years to come. They see the glorious moment when, like a warlock, Porter will end the ingrate of his choosing on this day of glorious judgment. His name will burn eternally. Children will cry when they hear his name. He will rule their nightmares. Porter sees them running. Porter sees them bleeding. He was the one who should have been worshipped. He was the one!

And then Porter Lanks sees himself dying. He feels the wondrous glory bleed out of him. Was it ever even there? He sees himself in the bathroom near the tech hall, alone as ever in his stall. The stall that still says, PORTER LANKS IS A FROG. It used to say, PORTER LANKS IS A FAG, but he spent a study hall period trying to carve something else—something that would still satisfy them, but something he could look at every day and not feel like he was already dead. He can see that when he's in the bathroom stall he won't be the king of a great carnage but something much lower, stupider than even a frog. People will remember his name—until they don't.

In the crowded halls of Wetmoss High, Porter reaches into his backpack and pulls out a slim notebook and pen and a biology textbook. Deirdra floats beside him as he walks to the bathroom near the tech hall. He goes into his stall, and he begins to cry, silently, the way he used to. For fun, he uses his pen to carve a small arrow pointing down between the words "a" and "frog" and writes "flying."

HOW TO SELL A JACKET
AS TOLD BY ICEKING

A mother and father and their two kids. Mother's eyes are on the PoleFace™ sign. There's a small smirk on my face, and I say, kind of to everyone but mostly to Mother, "What are we looking for today?" like I've been waiting for them my whole life. They look at me. And, because I saw how they came in, how their eyes pushed toward the back of the store, I already know what's coming when Mother says, "Well, um—" So I beat her there. "The best sale we have in the store right now is on our winter coats and jackets." She says, "That's what I like to hear." And we might as well mark up the sale right there.

"Seventh and tenth in the entire nation, so clap it up for that," Angela, the store manager, announced. The whole store flapped their hands at us. I watched them clap.

I've been top ten in the nation for two years straight. There's a good chance this year I'll crack top three in company history. Total sales. Still, it's a strange thing when a bunch of people

—some you like, some you hate all over again every shift—are clapping for you. And you have to kind of smile a little bit but not too much, as if to say, *Yes, I am, in fact, the shit.*

While they clapped, Florence smiled her perfect smile. I watched her, too.

Her second week in the store, Florence made a girl who came in for a hat for her boyfriend leave with a new fall wardrobe. Florence started not even a year ago. She's what some might call a natural, but really, I taught her a lot. Now when girls come in looking for jeans, they ask, "Is Florence in today?" like only Florence can divine the necessary denim for their begging hips.

Still, it's me Angela uses when she needs an example of what to do right. Even though, when she's talking about how to be a good employee, everybody knows I don't do any of the things she's talking about—except sell. In the mall the only truths that matter are the kinds you can count. Sales goals, register tills, inventory. Numbers are it. Everything else is mostly bullshit.

I'm lead sales associate because of my numbers. When managers step out to grab food, or smoke, or fuck in the shipment bay, they point to me, and say, "Hold the floor down." Sometimes they'll hand me a clipboard with everybody's break times and daily goals. Whenever I'm on the clock, my daily goal is the highest. They think it motivates me.

The family follows me to the PoleFace™ section. I walk so quickly they have to work a little to keep up. "So, who are we trying to keep warm this winter?" I'm walking fast because, one, I don't want any distractions keeping us from where we need to be and, two, I don't want Florence to come around making suggestions and, three, I want the family to get used to living life at my pace. The youngest child is a small girl; you can't even imagine her as a teenager. The other kid is a pimply boy, maybe fourteen. I smile at the kids quickly. I set my jaw and keep a thoughtful look on when I make eye contact with Father. When I look at Mother, I imagine my own mother; I smile with all the love of the world in my eyes.

Our store is basically a big warehouse with hangers and racks. We have clothes popularized by rappers and skateboarders. Families like this one are why I'm ranked nationally: two kids, still happy enough to shop together, white. Very American dream–ish.

"We're thinking about a coat for me and maybe this one," Father says out of the side of his mouth while gesturing toward the son who's drifting off toward the graphic tees.

"Something that will last," Mother says definitively.

"Look at this!" the young girl says. She pulls a blue shirt off a table. The shirt has a green moose on it. We stop to turn to the small child. I smile at her, then wait.

"Put that down," Mother says.

"But—"

"Leah," Mother says in that tone doctors must gift to new parents right after they have their first kid.

Leah's smile melts. She starts to toss the shirt back.

"A bunch of our best outerwear comes with a gift card as part of our winter sale," I say. Leah stops in her tracks. She smiles. She whips her look to Dad's eyes, then Mom's, and then back to Dad's, waiting for a face that says yes.

"Oh really?" Mother says.

"Yup," I say.

We're back on track to PoleFace™. Leah is throttling the blue shirt, then wearing it like a boa. When her parents aren't looking, I wink at her and we share a big smile. We pass the front register where Angela is standing guard and working backup.

I feel her eyes as I lead the pack to the winter section. My section. It's my break time, but Angela knows to let me work.

I take extra time on my breaks. When I'm not on break, I'll go to the bathroom and I'll sit on the toilet doing nothing for fifteen minutes sometimes. Every few minutes I flush the toilet so I can listen to the water escaping. The district manager treats me to pizza when he visits. He doesn't have to ask what I like anymore: two pepperoni slices and an iced tea. Most people get all nervous when they hear Richard is coming in—me, my mouth waters. That's his name, Richard. Nobody calls him anything else to his face. I can't remember the last time Richard called me by my name. He calls me IceKing. Every time he sees me, it's "There he is, the mighty IceKing." He started calling me that after my second Black Friday, a particularly gruesome one, where I doubled my expected total. He said I was IceKing because I was the lord of the winter sale season. I don't call Richard anything, even though over one of our lunches, he said, "Call me Rich. I'm not there yet, but a guy can dream, right?" He laughed, and I made myself laugh the same way he did.

"So this is everything." I motion with my arms, like, *Welcome to my humble abode.* There are thin jackets and fleeces on floor racks. Ski jackets and heavy coats hang like limp bodies from face-outs in the walls. There are even tiny jackets for infants. "What do we need?" I say to the family. Reminding them they need something.

"Thanks, buddy, I think we're okay to just browse around," Father says.

"He needs something for when we go skiing," Mother says

with a sigh. "In Denver," she adds, like she's letting some big secret out. I keep my smile low.

"That's great. This whole section here"—I walk a few steps; they follow—"is designed specifically for skiers and snowboarders." I stop in front of these jackets that have bright colors accented by reflective silver. They look like speed. They are thinner than a lot of our other stuff, and they are some of the most expensive pieces in the store. But this family can afford to see. I know what a desperate mother sounds like. This mother doesn't need a sale, but she considers herself a smart shopper. They are a happy family. I am IceKing.

If anybody has what I have, it's Florence. She is like me. Angela says Florence practically filled out her application while in labor. That's why she's so good. She's a mom even though we're both young enough that working here isn't automatically depressing—you have to think you're stuck for it to be. Also, Florence is pretty. Me, I got words and a smile. I wear clothes that show kids I know what's up. I hook a snapback hat so it hangs through the loops of my jeans. Florence can do all that *and* she's pretty. She has deep dimples. Her hair is always doing something amazing. When the cashiers ask, "Did anyone help you out today?" customers say, "The one with the nice hair," when they mean Florence. When they mean me, they say, "The tall one," if they're white. If they're black, they say, "The black guy."

A family like this one, it doesn't matter who actually needs anything. Mom is the mark.

"Hmm," Mother says, looking to me for a second opinion. The jacket Father has on is a credibility jacket. They need to see me not like something. Father is frowning, looking at his arms in the material. It's black and blue, and it happens to have the ability to completely transform into a backpack. I say this several times.

"I don't need anything fancy. It's just skiing," Father says. He didn't even want to come to the mall today.

"Yeah, now that it's on you, I'm not so sure about it," I say. Father looks at me and tries not to smile. "You have a bunch to choose from. This one might be better for your son, maybe."

"He can get whatever he wants." Father starts peeling himself free. "But I don't need a jacket that turns into a purse."

"Yeah," I say, chuckling like he does.

The wife folds her arms and waits for something to happen. While her husband wrestles out of the jacket, I look at Mother. She rolls her eyes. I do the same. Without words, together we say, *Men make everything so difficult.* Then, as I'm taking the jacket from a still-grumbling Father, I look at him like *Women, am I right?*

"What about me?" the little girl with the blue shirt says. Mother and Father both slam looks at her. Leah frowns silently. I flash her a smile, and she flashes a bigger one back.

"I think . . . " I look around and settle on the coat. It's thick and olive green. It is heavy, but I'll say this explicitly, it's got vents that keep the material breathable. "Yeah, I think this one is the one." I know it's the one. I saw Father's eyes linger on it as he tried on the first jacket. I know Mother will like it because it looks expensive. It is expensive, though slightly cheaper than the credibility jacket. I can upsell. I can downsell. I can do it all.

"I'll try that one," Father mumbles. They don't have to tell me the size. With the first coat, I grabbed a large because they run a little bit bigger. This time I grab an extra large. Instead of just handing him the coat like before, I hold it open for him and drape him in it, so his first memory of wearing it will be one of ease. "Thanks," he says. He zips it, unzips it, shrugs his shoulders once, twice. Then he looks at his wife. Working here, I've learned that married men use their wives as mirrors.

Florence has sold three winter coats today already. Florence is currently seventh in the nation in sales. She's the real deal, but I'm me. I carve ICEKING in the walls of the shipping halls. That way, even when I'm done with the mall, my legend will live forever.

Father is waiting for Mother to say yes, but then he sees she's looking at me. I smile and nod, then circle Father once, pretending to be inspecting closely for some minor detail we might have overlooked. They're both watching me as I orbit. "I think this is the one," I finally say.

"I do, too," Mother says immediately. Father goes to look at himself in a mirror. Leah tugs at a jacket on a hanger. The young boy, he's just drifting back to the group.

"You think it's okay?" Father asks.

"Yeah, it's simple but clean looking, and it definitely looks solid," I say. I've said the same thing, the same way, to so many different faces.

"Mmhmm, you can tell it's quality," Mother says.

"How much is this thing going to run me?" Father says as he grabs the red tag dangling from the front zipper. He frowns deeply.

If it's a family that won't pay for the PoleFace™ after I show them the price, they'll say something like, "You're shitting me, right?" or "Okay, but what's the real price?" Right away, I say, "I know. Crazy, right?" Like it was a big joke. I'll rush to the cheaper stuff. I have about thirty seconds before they disappear. But before they're gone, I'll show them — "This here," another jacket of equal quality and half the price, "is what I wear when I'm upstate, in Albany."

"Albany?"

"Yeah, I visit a lot. I'm going to school up there." A wish. A lie. I don't know. "It's freezing," I'll say.

"You don't say," they'll say back.

"That's a whole lot to ask for one jacket," Father says.

"Well, part of it is the lifetime warranty," I say. "And—" Then, of course, Florence appears. "And right now," she says, "we're doing a new sale where for purchases of more than two hundred dollars on any combination of coats or jackets, you get a gift card back." She's holding a clipboard. She stands there, and you can feel the family deciding who they want as master. "Want me to toss that one behind the register for you while you look for another?" Then Florence turns to me. She says, "Angela told me to tell you to go on break." Her voice is sweet and acid. I stand for a second. Today they officially promoted Florence. Her name tag, where it used to say SALES AS-SOCIATE, says ASSISTANT MANAGER.

Last Black Friday, I sold almost eighteen thousand dollars' worth of coats, fleeces, and jeans by myself. It was a store record. Also, they had a contest that year. Whoever sold the most got a PoleFace™ item. I got my mom a jacket. It didn't fit right. She hardly wears it. Richard bought me an entire pizza. I didn't share it with anybody in the store. I ate one slice waiting for the bus. I held the greasy box on my lap for the ride. That was my big prize for the day until they could work out the paperwork for my coat. I ate one more slice then, when the bus stopped and I got off, I left the pie with a guy sleeping on cardboard outside the station. I like to remind Angela and Richard and Florence and whoever's around that I won't be here forever. I can sell, but I am not one of them. Whenever they try to get me to do extra stuff, I have to remind them that even though this is what I do best soon I'll be doing some other thing even better.

I think of saying, *Oh, I actually just came from break,* to Florence. But I am tired. I've worked a long time. I look at the family and Florence. I say, "Well, all right, guys, Florence here will help you out." I look for some sadness in the eyes of Father and Mother. They're looking at Florence.

"Well, I think I'm going to take this," Father says like he had a choice.

"Are you sure we can't do anything about the price?" Mother says.

"Well, if you think your son might like some of these ski jackets," Florence says, "we do have an additional deal for multiple significant purchases."

Florence was late twice during her first week. Angela told her a third strike was a third strike no matter how good she was. Five minutes before Florence was supposed to punch in that weekend, my phone buzzed. I was sitting in the bathroom, listening to the swirl and hiss of the water beneath me. *Flush, flush, flush.*

"Please, please, I need you. My babysitter was late. I need you to punch me in. I'm on my way, I'm coming, but I'll be late." All Florence's words had tears on them.

"Okay," I said. I tried to make my voice sound unmoved.

"That's it?" Florence asked.

"Yeah," I said.

"If Angela finds out—won't it be bad?"

"Not for me," I said. "And she won't. Tell me your username and password."

"They're both NaliaXO."

"All right," I said. Angela never found out. Before that, I thought me and Florence were the same. We are not. She's her. I am IceKing.

At the register, I punch out for break. Angela smiles warmly at the massive winter coat and the colorful jacket approaching in Florence's hands. The family trails her closely.

"Did anyone help you today?" Angela asks, sweetly.

"Absolutely, she even hauls the goods." Father chuckles as he points his thumb toward Florence. From behind the counter, I smile weakly at the family. Mother, Father, and Son look at me and see a stranger. Florence looks at us all and sees food. Leah looks at me and smiles a wide, crazy smile. Angela stares off toward the entrance, and says, "Hey, Richard. How are you today?" Richard's eyes bounce from Florence, to me, then back to Florence. My mouth waters.

IN RETAIL

n retail, if you don't wanna be a Lucy, you gotta find ways to make the bleak a little better. Lucy was that girl who jumped from the fourth floor last month on her lunch break. She used to be a cashier at Taco Town. Now she's a verb—"I'm gonna Lucy if today doesn't move any faster"—and a noun—"New girl never smiles. Looks like a Lucy." I try not to disrespect the dead. It's other people in the Prominent, from all different stores, who use her name a lot.

I've been here a while now, and the most important thing I've learned is that if you wanna be happy here in the Prominent Mall you have to dig happiness up, 'cause it's not gonna just walk up to you and ask you how you're doing. That is, unless somebody who doesn't speak the language walks up to you. That's different.

I love it when older Spanish ladies come into the store looking for something for their daughters, or sons, or nieces, or nephews, and none of the Spanish speakers are in, so they have to deal with me. I like it when they're older women because a lot of us younger types aren't so good at not being assholes to each other. I think having had money, and then having lost it, and had it again, and lost it some more, some older people kind of just say, *Screw it, I'm going to smile*. Maybe they're just too tired to be mean.

"Speak Spanish?" the lady will begin. She'll say that much in English. But even those two words she'll sing in a way English speakers just don't. Here, I'll close one eye, bring up my hand to measure out an inch of air between my thumb and pointer finger as I reply, *"Muy poquito."* I say it with a smile and a half laugh. She'll smile back, and say, *"Un poco inglés,"* and we'll both laugh as if to say, *I guess we'll meet somewhere in the middle*. She'll carry most of the burden. Her English is way better than my Spanish despite the fact that I got an eighty-six on the Spanish Regents in high school.

"Una camisa para . . . eh." She'll look around. And I'll jump in, like, *"Un niño o niña?"* And the lady's eyes will light up like blown coals, and she'll smile honestly and widely, and say, *"Niña, niña."* She'll tap you on your shoulder gently as a way of telling you how well you're doing. She'll be more excited than she has to be, and so will you. Pay attention to this moment. Suck it in like the last sip in the juice box.

Okay. So now, as we walk over to the women's side of the store, we'll be moving together in stride as if we've been friends for years. She might be saying a lot of words in Spanish now, and I'll understand almost none of them. But I will know she's being extremely friendly, and I'll enjoy the sound of her. If I'm lucky, I'll catch one of the words I've hung on to from those basic-level Spanish classes.

There's no way I deserved that eighty-six I got on the Spanish Regents. Ms. Ramirez, my teacher, was, at best, unorthodox and, at worst, absolutely bonkers crazy. She liked me because I pretended to believe all her insane stories.

She once told the entire class that her dog, one of those little living-accessory dogs that spends most of its life in a pleather handbag, hung itself by slipping through the beams of her deck after securing the other end of the leash beneath one of the patio chairs. She said it was proof that even animals could think and feel. I think she wanted us to become vegetarians. After she told that story, some kids asked her to elaborate—surely she didn't mean that her dog had literally hung itself because it was unhappy with the life she had provided for it. "Of course not!" Ms. Ramirez had said. It wasn't actually her dog. Her dog (Paprika) had loved her dearly. The dead-by-asphyxiation dog was actually her neighbor's dog (unnamed). At some point there had been a mix-up—well not exactly a mix-up but a switcheroo. Ms. Ramirez's neighbor, Sydney (a recurring villain in Ms. Ramirez's world), after seeing how much Paprika loved Ms. Ramirez, decided to get a dog of the same exact breed and size. When Sydney's tiny new dog didn't glow with the same delightful charm as Paprika, Sydney concocted and executed a scheme to switch the dogs, leaving Ms. Ramirez with an identical, though evidently psychologically troubled, mutt. Ms. Ramirez decided to allow the switch to happen without saying a word. "But why, Ms. R?" we'd asked as a class. How could you let that happen? And then she took off her glasses like she always did when she wanted more drama and used her other hand to point at her chest as she said, *"Mi corazón es grande."*

So Ms. Ramirez was not all there, but I got on her good side and I set up camp. I laughed at the supposed-to-be-funny parts of her stories. I scowled when she mentioned Sydney's name. I treated her myths as history. She was pretty much talking to herself during the oral part of my exam, leaving me nodding and saying *"Sí"* while reaffirming that, regardless of what she was saying, *"Mi comida favorita es pollo y arroz"* and *"Mi color favorito es rojo."* I think she needed us to do pretty well on the Regents to get tenure.

And so, as we're walking toward the women's side of the store and I'm listening to the chorus of Spanish I don't understand, I'll stop walking as this lady—who is, at this point, practically my best friend—says, *"Rojo."*

"Una camisa rojo, sí," I'll say with a triumphant smile. And the woman will practically jump in the air with happiness. She might grab my shoulder again. This time it'll be more than a tap. A hug of the hand. I'll just barely feel her nails through my T-shirt. We're like old friends now. The kind that know the worst about each other and don't always speak but check in enough and decorate the internet with pictures of each other's kids. Finally, we'll get to the shirts, and there'll be so many choices. I'll run my hand above them like there's a harp there and do a little dance. She'll clap and smile and then touch me once more on the shoulder, and say, *"Gracias, gracias,"* and she'll laugh. I'll laugh, too. Both laughs will taper off because we'll understand that this is the end of the road for us. We'll smile at each other, and I'll say, "Look for me if you need anything else," and she'll reply in her singing vernacular, "Okay, okay," and I'll walk off toward a mountainous wall of quarter-folded jeans that have to be counted before 12:30. Yesterday there were 1,598 pairs. Today there should be 1,595. We count them every day now since Richard is really trying to push on the loss-prevention side of things. Work is hard to find. There's a tiny angel at home who needs me, so I work for her. And I'm good at this, getting people to buy things. So I count.

I count the columns of jeans with my clipboard and pen to keep track. I count up each section then add the section totals together at the end. If what I get doesn't exactly match the computer inventory, I'll count them again, touching each pair of jeans, feeling the starchy blue denim pull the moisture from my fingertips. The Spanish lady sifts through the piles trying to find the perfect shirt. When she finally does grab a shirt she likes, you can see she's pleased from the way she glides to the register. She is going to make someone happy. You have to grab for happiness in places like this because there isn't enough to go around for everybody. Working retail is never gonna be the armed services or the police or anything. It's a job at least. It could be worse. Everywhere is different. Some places, people eat alcohol-infused chocolate-covered strawberries. Other places, everything tastes like cholera. The idea is that even in nothing jobs like this, you need to think of ways you might really be helping somebody, or you could end up a Lucy.

I hate using her name like that, but everybody in the mall does it. The best salesperson in our store told me not to think about it too much because pretty soon it would be somebody else. He said that every six months or so somebody takes the big dive. Before Lucy, he told me, it was Jenn from Radio Castle; before Jenn, it was Antoine who left Fleet Feet in the middle of his shift and fell backward from the railing, his hands still clasped in prayer. Lucy knows what gravity really is. Lucy went to knock on the door most of us pretend doesn't even exist. The day it happened the mall was in a frenzy, a lot of stores were doing a midseason BOGO sale. You'd have thought the circus was back—which would have been weird 'cause it had just left two weeks before; they'd set up in the G and H lots. They smelled like animal life and candy for two weeks.

Walking to the bus stop, I'd seen a bunch of people huddled around the railing. By the time I looked down, they'd already tossed a yellow tarp over her. You could see some red had seeped into the carpet around the yellow edges. And that wasn't the sick part. The sick part was looking up and down—my store is on the third floor—at the people pointing or snapping pictures with their phones. I remember thinking, I just hope she died on impact. And I hoped that wherever she was she remembered what those seconds before the ground were like. People said she screamed the whole way down, but I don't think she was afraid. I didn't know her name then.

Down below me that day, I saw two kids near Cone Zone joking with each other and, like, pretending to lean over and fall. They were only one floor above Lucy and her yellow blanket. You'd think the mall would maybe close for a few hours. Let people gather themselves. Maybe light a candle or something. Nope. Buy One Get One stops for no one. I held Nalia in my arms that night and fell asleep with her on the couch. When we woke up together that morning, her coo and cry made me forget some of the sick feeling I'd felt through the night.

Go back to counting jeans. Think about anything and count. Don't think about how a small part of you wishes you'd seen it. Her standing on the railing of the fourth floor. Lucy, flying. Count.

As I tally up the Levi's and think about how to not be Lucy, the beautiful lady who doesn't speak my language will appear behind me and tap me on the shoulder. Out of her bag, she'll pull a red shirt with some flowers outlined with gemstones on it. She'll show it to me. It will be so red that it will look like it might be hot to the touch. She'll say, *"Gracias, gracias,"* a few more times and tap my shoulder in parting, and I'll say, *"De nada, de nada,"* which will be a lie, because she is everything.

THROUGH THE FLASH

*Y*ou are safe. You are protected. Continue contributing
to the efforts by living happily, says the soft voice of the
drone bird hovering only a few feet from my window, as
it has been for the last forever. Since I'm the new me, I don't
even think about killing anybody. Still, I touch the knife under
my pillow.

Outside, a blue sky sits on top of everything, and I try to
think about it like this: Aren't we lucky to have our sky? Isn't it
an eternal blue blessing? Even though seeing it makes me feel
crushed a little because whoever's on the other side of time has
no idea how tired we are of the same.

I get up and I brush my teeth. It's the little things. Then I look
in the mirror, and say, "You are supreme and infinite." I take
my headscarf off and let my hair breathe. I spritz and moistur-
ize and finger-comb. The little things. After I'm dressed, I snap
on a gray fanny pack and put Mom's knife in it.

I jump out my window to a tree branch, then across to the
Quan family's roof, and then onto Mrs. Nagel's roof. I slip in
through her window, and her house smells like cinnamon and
old people as usual and always. In her kitchen I boil the water

for her tea. The kettle whistles. I make Mrs. Nagel 's favorite: elderflower and honey. I put the mug on her bedside and watch her sleeping uncomfortably. Her nose is stuffy, so she wheezes like an old truck.

"Hey, Mrs. Nagel," I say as gently as I can.

"Hey." She squirms in the bed a little, then opens her eyes. She sees me, and I like how she isn't terrified. She almost smiles even. "Thanks, Ama. I appreciate it," she says. I pick a box of tissues off the floor and give them to her.

"No problem, Mrs. Nagel. Have a good one. Remember, your existence is supreme."

"Uh-huh," Mrs. Nagel says. Then she blows her nose. I smile at Mrs. Nagel before I slip out her window and leap back home the way I came.

Inside, I pass by my little brother's room. He's awake in bed. I can tell by the sound of his breathing. His sheets have trains all over them.

"Hey, Ike," I say. That's short for Ikenna.

"Ama, please," Ike asks in his whiny voice. He wants me to end his day. He wants me to kill him. He didn't used to be like this. He was six when the Flash hit, so his body can't do all the things he wishes it could. He still has his small peanut head and cheeks you want to pinch. But I don't pinch; he hates his cheek pinchies now. That's another thing I have to think about as I'm being my new self. I am forever fourteen, and I can do more than anyone. I am blessed. But Ike's blessed in his own way. "Ama, goddamn it. Just do it for me, please," he says.

"Why? It's a great day outside," I joke. I've made that joke more times than—well, I've made it a lot of times.

"Do you hate me?" Ike asks. "You must truly hate me to deny me this."

No matter how much he's crammed in his head, when I see

him, I still see my kid brother. Ike's one of the ones who can't do it themselves; he's a softy.

"I love you," I say. Ike screams a bunch of bad words, but still I won't kill him because even the old me never did that. Not him. He doesn't leave his room much anymore. I let him be and go to the kitchen.

"Hello, Daddy," I say in a singing voice that sometimes makes him smile. My father is in his old-man slippers and his pajama pants. He is fidgeting, swaying, like always. He can't be still hardly ever. He's getting ready to cook something. Am I nervous around him? Yes. But I try not to be. Now that I'm the new me, I try to be appreciative. Appreciative and definitely not afraid. If I get afraid, then I get angry. If I get too angry, I might go back to being the old me and be just like Carl on Kennedy, who is a monster. A war god. A breaker of men and women and children.

"Morning, ginger root," he says. Then he turns to me, and he's holding the knife he uses to cut meat.

"Daddy," I say. Then he slashes at me with the butcher knife. I have enough time to think some real thoughts as his arm moves to my neck. I could open my pack, grab Mom's knife before Dad's blade reaches me. But I don't. Instead, I think, *When will this ever stop?* He's quicker than most people. But I'm faster than everyone. Way faster. Much more lethal when I want to be. The old me would make him suffer greatly. Instead, I try to say *Daddy* again but can't — not with my gashed-up neck and all — so I bleed out watching him watch me die. Then I die.

I'm in a gym, still in my jersey. Sweaty and upset. I feel a strong hand on my head. My face is crammed into her stomach. I can smell her along with the pinewood and dust of the Ramapo

Middle School gym. I can feel her. My mother rubs my neck. She says, "It's okay." Then pushes me off to the locker room where my team is waiting.

You are safe. You are protected. Continue contributing to the efforts by living happily. I wake up. I look around and try to decide if what I think just happened really did happen. I decide it did. I had a dream. I saw my mother in a dream. It's something new. New things never happen anymore. There are no dreams except the ones you had the morning of the Flash. I haven't had a dream in forever. And still, I saw my mother. She was really there with me. I want to see her again. I want to feel her again. I pull out my knife. Her knife. I stare at the blade, and I tell myself it's only this one time. It's only this one time and then never again. Then I drag the knife through my arm. I bleed and bleed. Then I go.

No dream. No mom. Regular.

You are safe. You are protected. Continue contributing to the efforts by living happily.

I wake up in the usual. Blue sky, in bed, knowing everything will be the same. But still, after my father killed me, I saw something I've never seen before. I dreamed a dream. That never happens. It wasn't there the next time, but still. I saw her. I jump out of bed.

"Ike!" I say, running up to his room.

"What?" he groans. "Are you going to help me or not?"

"I'm not going to kill you," I say. "But something happened." He knows me as well as anybody. Everybody knows everyone very well. We've all been together in the Loop longer than any group of people ever. But Ike knows me best. He gets out of bed and sits cross-legged on the floor. That's how he sits when he's thinking for real. That's how he sits when he cares.

"What happened?" he asks. And now he sounds like the old Ike.

"I had a dream," I say.

"So?"

"I mean I dreamed through the Flash. I didn't wake up, then take a nap and dream. I saw it before I came back. That's never happened before."

"Are you sure?" he asks. He grabs a little flip notepad with a purple pig on the cover and a crayon. "What did you see?" he says, and starts scribbling. Nothing he writes will last through the Flash—everything goes back to how it was the day the bomb dropped—but writing in it helps him think.

"Well," I say. "I saw Mom."

Ike gets up, takes a breath, and then sits back down. "Ama, tell me what you saw, exactly."

"I was with Mom. At Ramapo. I think it was just after the first game of the year. We'd lost, I guess. Even though in real life I think we won. All this was before; you probably can't remember. But she hugged me, and it made me feel better."

"I do remember," Ike says, like I hurt his feelings.

"Is this an anomaly?" I ask, finally.

Ike's crayon dances words down. "Perhaps," he says. He bites his lip. I wish I could share the dream better for him. I know he'd give anything to see Mom that way.

"Ama," my father calls. And my hands move toward where my fanny pack would be, but I'm still in my sleep shorts. "Sweetie?" he says. He's in my room. He knows how good I am at hiding. How I might be anywhere. I don't want to die yet. I'll be the old me if I have to be.

"What do you wanna do?" I ask Ike while creeping toward the door and out of the room.

"We'll definitely do something." And that's already the best because he hasn't wanted to do anything in a long time. "Let me think a little."

"Okay, I'm going to see Daddy," I say to warn him it might get bad.

"It's unlikely he'll be aggressive," Ike says without looking up from his notebook. "He'll want to apologize to you, I think."

"Daddy," I say. He's standing in his shorts and a T-shirt and his flip-flops. He has a stack of pancakes and juice on a tray in his hands. He always makes pancakes, which are my favorite, or crepes or omelets the cycle after he kills me. No matter how used you are to getting a knife whipped through your neck or punched in the eye or in the chest over and over again, it hurts. It's much better to end a cycle with the Flash, which doesn't hurt at all. Plus, you never know for sure that the Flash is coming even though it always, always does. And wouldn't that be a shame if your own father already had killed you the day the Loop broke and you actually would have had a tomorrow?

That's how the Loop affects him. He's basically a sad monster half the time. The other times he's my daddy. I try to love him either way. After he kills me, when the cycle restarts, he feels guilty. You'd think he'd eventually feel so guilty that he'd stop doing it. One day he'll be better, I hope. I know. The new me lets him do it most of the time. The old me made it a mission to end him way, way before the Horn came. But I'm the new me. And I'm trying to make him better. He wasn't always like this. He only kills me because I remind him of Mommy.

Sometimes he says her name while he does it. "Glory, Glory, Glory!" That's the sound of him killing me most times. Mom killed herself with her knife. My knife now. If she'd waited two months, she would have been with us forever. There aren't enough words for forever.

When he's standing there holding pancakes and trying to be better, I love him. It's not even that hard. "Thanks, Daddy," I say as I walk toward the bed and Mom's knife. I don't tell him about the dream because I don't know how it will make him act. If he's having a good day, I like to leave it alone. He puts the tray on my bed.

"How are you feeling?" he asks. He knows I can cut him to pieces.

"I feel infinite and excited and ready to do anything and everything," I say. I give him a hug.

"Great. I'm thinking maybe we watch the day end. Together. You know, on the wall."

"Def," I say. We don't talk about him cutting my neck open. He never apologizes with words, but he's always trying his best.

"Okay, Mama Ama," he says. Then he touches the tray again. To tease me, he genuflects before he leaves the room and walks back downstairs. When he's down there, he sits on the kitchen chair with the wobbly leg, and he starts to cry. I'm really good at telling where people are. I can almost see them just by paying attention to the sounds of a house. My senses are a blessing.

I take my tray of pancakes back to Ike's room. He's dressed in sneakers that light up when he steps and a blue T-shirt with a cloud that has a smiling face.

"I think this might be a legitimate anomaly, Ama," Ike says. "I want you to be sure, though; was it a dream sustained before you restarted the Loop, not something you thought of when you woke up?"

I look at Ike all dressed up. "Yes!" I say. I'm almost sure.

It didn't happen all at once. It was forever ago. I realized Ike was speaking like an adult. That was the first thing I noticed. That was the first thing that helped me put the days together. That's when I started keeping through the Flash. It's like realizing you're in a dream except no matter what you do you can't wake up. Daddy didn't start remembering through the Flash until much later. By the time I started to keep through the Flash, Ike was already smarter than everybody. That was the first anomaly, asymmetrical retention through Loop expiration, that he explained to all of us. Which meant, for reasons we still don't know, we each came to realize we were replaying the same thing over and over, and the realizing happened at different times for everyone. It was a pretty alarming thing. To see you're trapped in infinity and know that no one can explain exactly how or why.

We tried running, like maybe if we ran far enough we could escape.

There is no escape.

So, to ease the transition, we'd throw a party each time somebody kept through. Those were good times on the grid, the space we live in as designated by war-effort planning. The last one to keep through the Flash on Grid SV-2 was Mr. Tuia. We had a big party the day he came through. There was barbeque and music, and Ike danced, and the Poples danced, I danced, and Mrs. Nagel waved her arms from a lawn chair, which was like dancing for her, and my father laughed and laughed. Mr. Tuia mostly cried. It's very hard at first for some people. But then if you figure that you are infinite, you are supreme and therefore the master of all things, and it's silly to be sad about things like how much your hip is always going to hurt or how you're so old that the flu means life in a bed or how gone forever your mother is.

The second anomaly Ike and Robert, who was a marine biologist before the Flash, explained to us was how, individually, some of us were "developing and accruing attributes." Accumulating, they'd said. Some people were accumulating differently. Ike's brain was storing facts and stuff better than anybody's. Lopez on Hark Street was all right on the clarinet before, but now we're pretty sure he's the greatest musician to have ever lived. I got strong, fast, precise. I became the Knife Queen. We have a pretty interesting grid.

I don't know much about the other grids in our state block, because way before the Flash came, the soldier-police—the state-sponsored war-coordination authorities—took away everyone's cars. Their slogan—"For us to serve and protect, you must conserve and respect"—is emblazoned on posters in the school, on the windows of some people's homes. The Poples pretended they were proud when their son was shipped for service. The poster in their window shows the soldier-police slogan in big letters stamped below men with puffed-out chests proudly holding the flag and guns, their faces hidden by the black visors of their helmets. Back before the Flash ever came, a lot of people actually loved the SPs. They thought they were keeping us safe. People believe lies, believe anything when they are afraid. That's another thing. Aren't we lucky that before the Flash all the soldier-police were deployed elsewhere?

Still, even if you bike as hard as you can in any direction, only stopping to drink water, even if you pee and drink at the

same time, you can only get so far before the Flash takes you.
Even if you train for years and years. I've tried, and if anybody
should have been able to do it, it's me. I use my body better
than anyone. I can jump Olympic. I can break grown men with
my bare hands. When I have a knife, I'm basically the queen of
the world. Or the old me was. Now I let everyone be their own
royalty.

"I want to discuss this with Robert," Ike says.

Then the Horn comes. Three hundred and sixty-seven drone
birds all over the area screaming together. It's like a bright light
for your ears. It's the right sound for what it is. It means de-
fenses have been breached and the world is gonna end today. It
lasts for two minutes. One hundred and twenty seconds. I close
my eyes and wait. Ike does the same. Then it stops. The Horn
is the exit point for many. It comes, and they just can't take the
sonic bleed. So they take whatever they have handy and jam it
into their neck. But if you close your eyes and breathe, if you
expect it and welcome it even, it's still terrible, but the kind of
terrible you can take.

The quiet after the Horn is sweet and lush. It's something
you don't want to let go of. But we have work to do. "Okay," I
say after we appreciate a few moments of silence. "Let's go see
Robert."

"I want to be inside before the rain," Ike says.

"Maybe we'll do that; maybe we won't. We're supreme and
infinite," I say, reminding him that rain is a small thing for infinite beings.

"Yes, so I've heard, Ama. I'd still like to be inside before the
rain," he says.

"I'll go grab the stuff."

"I'll be waiting." Ike pokes a fork into my pancakes.

I get ready in my room, then I jog downstairs and head outside. Two houses down I see Xander strangling his dog on their green lawn. It weeps and yelps, and its tail flaps around like a helicopter blade until it stops.

"Hello, Xander," I say with a big wave. Before, he had been a friend of my father's, and like my father, he was too old to fight. There aren't any men left from age twenty to forty-five.

"Hi there, Ama."

"What did poor Andy do today?"

"What do you mean?" Xander says, then he goes back in his house.

I knock once on the Poples' door. The big window where they keep their soldier-police poster gets smashed every morning, so the poster is facedown, hanging in the shrubs, dressed and stabbed with glass. It's the first thing the Poples do most days. Smash that window that reminds them of how gone their son is. When the door doesn't open fast enough, I kick it open. Mr. Pople is naked on his couch, drinking a glass of something. His skin is flappy and foldy.

"Hey, Mr. Pople."

"Ama Knife Queen Adusei," he says slowly, smiling and raising his glass and bowing his head.

"Just Ama," I say. Not in a way that's threatening, but just to remind him I don't make people say that anymore and haven't for a while.

"Ama," he says very slowly. He looks into his cup, then drinks from it. His hands head down toward his waist.

"See ya, Mr. Pople," I say as I run up the stairs. I go to his bedroom and grab the small piercer gun from a drawer. It's the first gun I ever shot. It's a small black thing with a smooth kick. It makes almost no sound when you pull the trigger. It kills in whispers, which I like. Or used to like. There's an extra clip in the same drawer. I grab both.

"Hello, Ama," says Mrs. Pople, who's still in bed, a cover up over her head.

"Hi, Mrs. Pople, gotta go," I say.

"Tell your brother to come see me soon."

"He's a little caught up today," I say and I don't mention that it's been a very long time since she and Ike were life partners.

"I see. He prefers Jen. Still?" Jen was a teacher at the school. But I don't know if Ike prefers anyone right now.

"You'd have to ask him, Mrs. Pople. But maybe your husband is interested? Or maybe Xander is. I think I heard him say he thought you were interesting and physically very attractive."

"You're a nice girl, Ama," Mrs. Pople says.

"We're all supreme and infinite. We might as well act like it," I say as I zip my fanny pack closed. I really am settling well into becoming a better person, I think. I've really come a long way from what I was, and I was once a true terror. The kind that probably never existed ever before. But now here I am, being called "nice."

Kennedy Street is down on the other side of the grid, so it takes a little while on the bike. Days are short. Soon it will rain, and Ike wants to be inside before the rain. "Bye, Mr. Pople," I say without looking at him doing whatever he's doing.

"Goodbye, my liege," he says.

My bike is on the side of our house. I run back in to tell Ike I'm ready, then wait for him outside. I do my kicks and my punches and some tumbles to get loose. I jump some jacks. I give the maple in our yard two good punches and a roundhouse kick to the trunk, and it crashes down. The sound of splitting wood excites me, I admit. It's different from the sound of snapping bones, but it reminds me of that kind of breaking. Then my father comes outside and looks at me. He has a glass of water in his hands.

"Thirsty?" he asks.

"Yeah, a little bit," I say. He extends his arm to me, and I walk toward him. I take the glass. It's cold, nice.

"Where are you going?" he asks like he might have before the Flash. Like he wants to tag along.

"Just riding around on the bike," I say. His eyes narrow a little, then he takes a deep breath and relaxes.

"Okay," he says. He turns around, and Ike slides past him outside.

"You, too, Ike? You're out of bed? You're going outside?"

"Yes, I'm looking forward to some fresh air," Ike says.

"That's spectacular," my father says. It's been a long time since Ike has been outside. "You riding with Ama?" my father asks. He sounds so excited that it's almost like he's the father I had when I had a mother—that person I only sort of remember. The one who would hold me by my feet and tickle me until I couldn't breathe. I remember that fun, breathless struggle. I also remember, always, that he didn't treat my mother well. He used to yell and scream. I used to hide in my room with Ike, and to distract him, we'd play hide and seek. Back before Ike was a genius. Before I was a murderer. That I remember.

"See ya, Daddy," I say, and give him a hug. I keep my eyes open all through it.

"Have fun, ginger root," he says as he touches my hair. And I close my eyes for a half second to feel the simple good of his hands on my head. Then I'm on the bike, and Ike is sitting in front on the handlebars, and we're riding in the wind like we're unstoppable beings who truly have all anyone could ever hope for.

Our street is Harper, and then we ride down Flint to get onto Conduit AB-14, which we stay on for a while. Conduit AB-14 is framed by trees full of drone birds and dirt. It's four lanes of empty road. Naked road for miles and miles, and if it didn't mean the end of the world, all that empty might be beautiful, maybe.

On the way we see a group of men and women beating down some other man. When I ride by, they stop to look at me. I smile and wave. When they see me, their eyes go wide, then the group of them run off in the opposite direction. "I'm not gonna hurt you," I call out. They don't believe me. They don't stop running. The one who was getting beat on gets up. His face is mashed pretty good. "You're still magnificent and supreme. Nothing can change that," I tell him. He picks up a rock. Turns from me, unbuckles his pants, and shows me his butt cheeks. Then, when his pants are back on, he goes running after the group.

"Meatheads," Ike says, trying to keep me from feeling bad.

"Yeah," I say.

It takes us almost an hour to get there. I stop two streets before Kennedy to catch my breath, and we walk the rest of the way. Carl's cluster looks pretty much like ours, but it's quieter. People mostly stay inside here because of Carl.

"I think the furthering of variance might truly suggest the dissolving of consistency we've always expected," says Ike.

"Hope so," I say. And we walk more.

When we finally do get to Kennedy, the heads of two women, Patricia Samuel and Lesly Arcor, are stuck onto the street sign. Carl's set the two heads up to look like they're kissing. Patricia Samuel is Carl's mother.

"I guess Carl is still Carl," Ike says. Looking around, curious, kind of scared, almost like how I imagine a real little kid might look. There are no more real little kids. Even the babies know they're stuck. Most of them don't cry at all. Some of them never stop crying ever.

It always looks like World War VI over on Kennedy because of Carl. Two houses are on fire. There are dark spots that show where Carl's victims bled out on the streets. He's a real terror. Still. It's easy to judge him because, I mean, he does the absolute worst stuff to people. I once saw him use his body and various household objects to physically violate eight people, who were all tied up at once. He was fourteen when the Flash came, like me.

It's supereasy to think he is the Devil himself because of all the things he does and because sometimes he screams, "In this hell, the Devil, the Lord, and everything in between is named Carl," but I've been there. Being strong can make you like that. Carl is my protégé. He'll never admit it, but it's true. He's the protégé of Knife Queen Ama. The Ama who started with one knife and ended with three blades and two guns, who could kill all one hundred and sixteen people on my cluster in one hour and twenty-two minutes. I'd take a shower and change halfway through because my clothes got so heavy. Every inch of my black skin painted the maroon of life. The old Ama would murder everyone because, when everyone was gone, she got to feel like she was the only one in the world and there was no one who might ever do her wrong again. Sometimes she'd just sit in the grass and feel supreme and infinite. She'd try to stare at a single blade of grass, or dance in the empty streets, or sing at the top of her lungs, until the Flash came. Sometimes she'd cry and cry as she washed the blood from her hair and eyes. Sometimes she wouldn't wash it off at all.

Imagine the worst thing anyone has ever done. I promise, I've done it to everyone. More than once.

When I realized I was faster and stronger, at first I didn't know what to do. I thought that maybe I was supposed to be on top now. I thought I was getting rewarded. And so I did what I wanted. Before the Flash, Carl was not nice to me. He liked to call me "nappy-headed bitch," or "dumb-ass cunt." He liked to make me cry back when we still had school. Then, when my mother left us, when I saw him, he said, "Guess your mother didn't want to be alive, knowing she made you." That, well, I know he regrets saying that. Because after the Flash, once I realized what I could do, I hunted him. He was the first person I ever killed. He was the first person I'd kill every day. The hurt I've pulled out of that boy could fill the universe twice over.

I'd rush over to his house and find different ways to ruin him. There is nothing—nothing—I haven't done to Carl Samuel. I know well-done Carl from medium-rare Carl. I made sure his mother knew the difference, too. Even made her choose a favorite. It was a good day for me when she admitted her preference.

"Tell me, Patricia, which do you prefer?" I laughed. She was tied to the posts on the side of the stairs. I grabbed her cheeks. Her son's blood was crusting beneath my fingernails. I pulled her face down to the two strips of meat I'd cooked just a few minutes before. I fried the boy's arm pieces in olive oil. I even added salt, pepper, and adobo. Carl was writhing and crying behind me. His arm severed and the wound cauterized. I didn't even have to tie him up.

"Hey, baby. You are supreme and—" Mrs. Samuel started, and then I snapped one of her fingers. She screamed. By then, I was immune to the sound of humans screaming. Or the thing I think others felt when they heard someone hurt, I felt the exact opposite. It was music for me: the way people scream when they're just afraid versus when they *know* their life is going to end. The unrelenting throaty sobs a man makes when you dangle his life in front of him, the shouts a child makes as you remove their arm. The sharp harshness that comes from a mother who can't save her son and can't stop trying. But that day Patricia Samuel swallowed up her scream and stared past me to her son. "You are infinite; this is nothing. I love you, Carl. You are perfect. You are supreme. You are infinite. We are forever."

"Very sweet. Now tell me, Mrs. Samuel." I smiled and made my voice soft. "Do you prefer the well-done or the medium?" Patricia Samuel wept as I turned my back to her.

"Please, Queen Ama, I beg you, please spare him today."

"Knife Queen Ama," I corrected. "If you tell me which you prefer, I may find some mercy for you." I took the knife out of my fanny pack.

"Please, Knife Queen." She wept, just as desperate as a person can be.

I shook my head. "Carl, your mother did this to you," and then I pressed my knee on his neck. It's not that hard to remove someone's eye.

Carl's screams: yippy and small, and then they grow. They're wordy and pathetic. "Ah! Hey! Okay! Okay!" Like I was giving him a wedgie. Then they grow and pull and stretch. "Nooooo, nooooooo!"

"I love you, baby; it's okay," Mrs. Samuel said.

"Yeah, Carl, it's okay," I said, stabbing deeper, shucking the blade into the boy's skull. Laughing at how easy it was.

Carl was silent. He wasn't dead. His body shook.

"Please, Knife Queen!" She screamed for her son.

"Which do you prefer?"

"Ama, please!"

"Medium or well-done?"

So much misery in that room.

"Neither!"

"You have to pick," I said, looking up at her, smiling with her boy and so much of his blood in my hands.

"I—"

"In a second there'll be a very rare option on that plate," I said.

"Baby, I promi—"

"You *have* to pick," I repeated. It was like holding down a fresh-caught fish.

"Mom!" Carl screamed.

"Well-done," she finally said.

I stopped. "Take another bite to make sure." She followed my command immediately. Bending down, almost breaking her own arm to eat the meat with her mouth as her hands were tied to the posts behind her.

"Well-done, Knife Queen Ama."

"Good to know," I said. "That's how you'll have your Carl next cycle."

Then I got up and left.

I forced Carl and Patricia to live similar nightmares hundreds of times. What's surprising is how it never got easier for them. Carl was always terrified; his mother was always desperate, destroyed, and ready to be destroyed for him.

I hunted Carl for so long that even though I still hated him I got bored. I started hurting other people. At first I only bullied the bullies. The people who tried to hurt. And then I started hurting everybody. The way I felt about Carl sort of leached out. I was a real terror. People accumulate differently. When Carl's body started accumulating like mine, when he got as strong as I was, as fast as me, as good with sharp things, then he became a real genuine terror, too.

There's dark red streaked everywhere on Kennedy. It's like walking into an old room you haven't lived in for a long time.

"Maybe let's get back on the bike," I say.

"Wise," Ike says, and then, as he's climbing up onto the handlebars, there's a bang. I look down and I don't have a knee anymore. It's just a shattered bloody thing. I eat back the screams I feel because I'm not the kind of person who screams anymore.

"Dammit!" Ike says. "We have to go."

"Sheesh," I say. "Okay, we're okay. We are—"

"Ama, I know, we have to go!"

Then Carl's screams from above us. "How dare you! *Sliht baree ki lopper TRENT.*"

When I realized that Carl was also accumulating in his body, that he was becoming like me and maybe had been like me the whole time but wasn't smart enough to realize it, I let him be my friend. Here in the forever Loop anything can happen. You can make a friend of the Devil. You can pretend everything was a dream. Carl was my only friend for a while. We did what we wanted to other people. We hurt them together. We even invented our own language: Carama. There are a lot of bad words in Carama. It's a language for war gods, so it's pretty aggressive. We've sat on rooftops and watched without fear as entire communities joined together to try to bring us down. *"Sliht baree ki lopper trent,"* he screams again. It means something like "Prepare for a violent death, you lowly creature."

"Just checking in," I say. "We're leaving."

"Ama!" Ike screams. I can see he's afraid, and he should be. But I haven't seen Carl in such a long time, and there's a chance that even he is different now.

"Checking out, actually," Carl says. And I hear him laugh at what he thinks is clever. He flips down from the roof of a house to the street. He's holding his piercer rifle. That's one thing.

When he starts his day, Carl has some pretty serious stuff ready
in his house. His father, before he died, was some kind of Aqua
Nazi. Even before the Water Wars started, he was preparing
against Black people, Middle Eastern people, Christians, and
Jews because he thought they were going to steal from the water reservoirs or something. He was a pretty mean guy, I guess.
Carl used to come to school black-eyed and bruised. Kids used
to laugh at how crazy his pops was. He wasn't a happy boy.
He's still not a happy boy. He wears a T-shirt on his head with
the neck hole slanted to cover his left eye, and the shirt's arms
are tied back in a knot behind his head. He uses an elastic band
he cuts from a pair of underwear like a headband over the shirt
to keep it in place even better. It's the first thing he does every
day. His eye, his eye. Some pain lasts through a hundred deaths.

The hot rain starts falling. Blue sky, Horn, hot rain, Flash.
Those are the totems. Those are the things that come no matter what you say, think, pray, do, or die. The hot rain feels like
a warm shower. Ike says the rain is a thermonuclear by-product
of all the bombing that was going on during the time the Flash
first hit. He says that even if the Flash didn't come the rain
would give us all cancer. But I like it. Every day it comes and
it's warm and it reminds you like, hey, wasn't that pretty good
when you were dry earlier?

"Kia Udon Rosher, ki twlever plumme sun," I scream, which
means, like, "Oh great destroyer, you are supreme." The feeling
in my mangled leg is disappearing, and the world starts flick-
ering out.

Carl laughs. He wears a purple bathrobe that belonged to
his father like the gun he raises.

"You're a stupid cunt," Carl says in plain old language. I feel
my old self in my fingers as I reach for my pack. He skips toward me as my knee bleeds and bleeds. It hurts very badly. I've

felt much worse, but it's so hard to remember anything other than what's now when you're hurt now.

After Carl and I broke our war-god pact and our friendship, we became sworn enemies. It happened because Carl didn't like how I acted like I was stronger than he was. Also, I think, because he was bored. One day he caught me off guard and knocked me out with a shovel. When I woke up, I was chained to a tree and I didn't have any fingers on my left hand. I was, like, "Sheesh." That was the beginning of a very, very long day. It had been lifetimes since anyone had been able to hurt me like that, and I realized how bad I had been, and for how long, and how I wasn't going to do anything like that ever again.

But now, with my knee exploded, I'm thinking about how I want to make Carl sip broth made from his own bones. I point the gun at my brother. Even after all this forever, it's something I do not like to do. Even if it's to save him from Carl, who will do things so, so much worse. Even the old me didn't kill Ike. Which is probably why he had such a hard time for a while. It was lonely for him: a boy in a dead town and his sister the bringer of all pain.

"No you don't!" Carl says, and I try to pull the trigger. There's a bang and it's not from my hands and then the world disappears and I leave my brother in the hands of the worst person on the planet.

You are safe. You are protected. Continue contributing to the efforts by living happily.

I wake up. I grab Mom's knife and hold it in my hands.

Good torture feels like it will never end. You never forget it. I wonder what happened to Ike as I brush my teeth and shower and stuff my knife into my fanny pack. Carl is great at torture. Carl knows what he's doing because Carl learned from me, and

I might be the best ever at that stuff. I imagine what Carl did to Ike, and I know he's been through the kind of pain that will never leave him.

I go to Mrs. Nagel's place. She's just so fragile and weak. Still. Always. Her breathing sounds like struggle, and even though she's sleeping, there are lines around her eyes like she's concentrating hard on something. I open my fanny pack and take out the knife. I put the blade against Mrs. Nagel's neck. The metal reflects a sliver of light against her skin as her throat grows and shrinks, carrying air in and out of her body badly. It'd be so easy even if she weren't so sick. She was the easiest out of everyone. She only woke up when the old me wanted her to. When I wanted her to know what was happening to her, which was a lot of the time. I take my knife back, tuck it into my pack, and go downstairs.

I squeeze lemon into elderflower tea. When I climb back up the stairs, Mrs. Nagel is awake, and she looks at me with eyes that are tired and warm. I put the hot mug on her nightstand.

"Ama," she says, and she scoots up in her bed. She tries to take a deep breath, but can't. She smiles and motions for the box of tissues that is always on the floor. Such a big difference it would make if it was just on her nightstand, if she could just have that one thing be easy and simple. Instead, that little thing, it's magnified by a million, and it makes you just want to cut your own head off that she can't just have that one thing be right for once.

"Hey, Mrs. Nagel," I say.

"What's wrong?" she says. It chills me to hear her ask. Even though it's been a long time, not a lot of people say things like that to me. Most people are afraid of me. A lot of them hate me and they should.

I climb up on the bed behind Mrs. Nagel so she can lean

back into me and I can massage her temples to help with the headaches. I say, "I feel like maybe I liked the old me better. The old Ama. It was easier. And maybe the new Ama isn't doing anything."

Mrs. Nagel blows her nose. "New Ama?"

"Yeah, you know. Me now," I say. "Like how I'm not killing everybody or torturing anyone or whatever."

"And that was the old Ama who did that?"

"Yeah."

"And what's the difference between the two?"

"The old me did everything one way. And only thought about one person. Now I try to help everybody instead of killing them."

"I see, but what changed?"

"I used to be afraid," I say. I watch her breathe and listen to see if her heart is beating faster, if she is afraid. She is not. "I know I can't take it back. I know I'm the worst person who ever lived. I know that. I'm not afraid anymore. I'm only scared of me."

"I see, and that means you've been two people?"

"I'm better now. And I'm sorry. But sometimes something in me—like right now, it'd be so easy." I continue to rub softly, but it's true. I can't stop imagining how easy it would be to crush Mrs. Nagel's neck. Like crumpling a piece of paper. "I'm sorry; I didn't mean that," I say. "I want everyone to feel happy and supreme and infinite. That's the new me."

"Hmm," Mrs. Nagel says.

"How can you not see the difference?" I say, trying to keep my voice down. "I'm so much better now. I am."

"I think you've done a fine job. People come visit me so often since you changed. And it's true that in the past you were a terrible witch."

"Exactly."

"But I think there's only one Ama. And I think I'm talking to her."

"I'm sorry. For all of it," I say.

"You should be." Mrs. Nagel points to the bathroom, which means she wants me to give her a towel with warm water for her head. I do it. Then we're quiet for a long time. I sit with her through the Horn. Then she falls back asleep. I sit with her for a while more. When I jump back home, the sky is already gray and the hot rain is already falling. Also, a bike I know belongs to Carl is set down on the grass. All the bikes on Kennedy belong to Carl. I pull my knife out. I climb up and slide inside my bedroom window and creep downstairs. Carl is sitting at the table. My father is making pancakes, swaying at the stove. And Ike is at the table, too, with his legs crossed in his chair and his back to me.

"There she is," my father says. I'm thinking I have the angle: I can leap across the kitchen table and get to Carl.

"Why is he here!" I say. "Ikenna, I'm sorry, I tried."

"Don't worry, I was fine," Ike says.

"You got to the gun? You got out?" I ask.

"No, I told Carl I had some info for Robert and he let me go see him."

"*Udon Rosher Carl jilo plam,*" Carl says. It means "Carl, the great destroyer, spared the weakling." He is in his robe with the shirt over his head. His one exposed eye stares at me and only me.

"Oh," I say.

"It's been so long. I asked Carl if he wants to watch the Flash with us. Remember when we used to do that. Remember, we would watch on the wall?" my father asks.

"Why are you here now?" I ask. I've gotten close enough that I know I have a good shot at him.

"I'm here to kill you and make your family watch," Carl says. I can see his hunting piercer is at his feet. My father turns and stares at Carl.

"Carl," my father says. "You used to be an okay kid. If I could, you know what I would do to you?"

"Yes, sir," Carl says.

"Okay," my father says. It's true. With me and Carl, it's better not to try to stop us when we want to do something. Everyone knows that by now. I smile because my father defended me and has been killing me less and less lately.

"What did Robert say?" I ask while I still can.

"Whatever happened with you," Ike says. "Whatever happened—you're the first it's happened to, so we'll see. Maybe it's a domino in an eventual collapse." We're all pretty quiet. "Nothing new, really. But we think we can say for sure that this isn't going to last forever. Unless it does."

"Okay," I say. And I leap. I lunge with my knife, and nobody else in the history of the world would even flinch, but Carl is Carl, so he grabs the table and flips it up like a shield. I use my elbow to blow through it pretty easily. The table is in pieces, and Ike runs back. My father stops cooking and swings a hot, pancakey pan at Carl. Carl ducks it, and as he does, I swing my knife at his neck. He dodges two good slashes, then kicks me hard in the ribs. I crash back into the dishwasher. Rib broken for sure. I get up and focus. I smile because I, Ama Grace Knife Queen Adusei, am a fighter, the greatest ever. Lately, I don't get to fight much. Or now I fight differently. But these fights, with fists and knives, I have more practice in. I jump forward again. Carl grabs my wrist and twists so I drop my knife.

"You are supreme and infinite, Carl, and I am very sorry for all that I have done," I say as I knee him in the ribs, and before even bringing my leg back down, I'm in a backflip and kicking into his chin. He stumbles back.

"BITCH!" Carl screams, and makes to grab the gun out of the rubble that's forming out of the kitchen. I kick him in the gut and throw him out toward the living room.

"Sorry, *Udon Rosher,*" I say while charging. He punches me in the mouth, and I see black, then the world comes back to me. "I meant no disrespect. I know you're strong. I just want you to know I am sorry for the things I did to you."

"Fuck you," Carl says, and he's coming at me with his flurry of heavy punches. He misses with a big right, and his fist goes through the wall. As he tries to pull his arm out, I get behind him and punch down on his neck in a way I know will make him crumble. Then I rip off the shirt on his head, and it's like I hit the master switch. *"Hellio YUPRA! Ki Udon Rosher! TRENT!"* Carl screams as he holds his eye. Weeping on his knees. "Okay! Okay! *Hellio yupra.*" Even when I'm not touching him, he screams and claws at his own eye. He becomes a little bit of the old Carl. I hit him another time, hard at the base of his neck, to keep him from moving. His paralyzed body does nothing, and his face keeps doing so much.

"Udon Rosher, ki love, okay," I say.

"End it!" Carl screams, keeping one eye open. Outside, the hot rain has stopped. I drag Carl upstairs and make sure he's comfortable in my bed. He screams and screams in Carama, and I understand him very well. He spits and cries. I sit with him. "I know you're going to get through all this," I say. When his voice is coarse and he can't scream anymore, I leave him.

My father and brother are in Ike's room. Ike is writing something. My father is coloring in a coloring book. "Ama!" my father says.

"Ama," Ike says.

"We're good," I say. My rib is broken, and I'm kinda bleeding out of my ear. "Still want to go watch?" I ask. These are my guys. I'm blessed knowing I can protect them.

Outside, the hot rain makes the air smell like burning rubber, but you can still smell the fresh wet earth underneath so it's not all bad. Once we were all keeping things through the Flash, it became a tradition for everyone on our street to watch it together, to disappear all at once. Then we stopped doing that.

We press ourselves to the side of our house facing west. I'm dizzy and happy. Breathing hurts, but still I feel as infinite as ever. Still supreme. We get on the wall. Our wall. I lean my back against it, and I feel the wet seep through. A long time ago, Ike explained to us how nuclear radiation, besides destroying stuff, bleached everything it didn't make disappear and that our bodies, if they were right up against something, would leave shadows that would last forever. For a long time we tried to use our bodies to send messages to the future. Hoping that after we were gone, if the Loop broke, the future would see us and know. I'd make little hearts with my hands, or sometimes we'd all hug each other to show them, like, love was a thing even for all of us who lived through the wars that ended everything. Now when we do it, it's mostly for fun.

"What are you going to do?" my father says.

"I think I'm going to do this," Ike says, looking up at us. He does a thing where he spreads his legs a little wider and acts like he's flexing both arms above his head. That's my brother. He's not too smart to be fun sometimes.

"Okay," my father says. "I'm going to do the animal man."

He grabs a branch from the maple I snapped and puts it on his head so he'll look like he has feathers. The future will think he's an alien. Me, I've already picked one leg up and tucked it into my knee. It's pretty hard to breathe, but it's not that hard.

"Dancer," I say before he asks. That's kind of my signature. I've done different versions of it, but this one is the best I can do with a broken rib and a knocked-around head. I have one leg on the ground, and then I bring one arm and crane it above my head. We only have to wait a minute.

There's a faraway light. Then a roar like long, slow thunder. The roar doesn't stop; it gets louder, and then it's so loud you can't hear anything. The faraway light grows, and it's yellow-ish at first, and in the beginning, it looks like something that's meant to help you, like another sun. Then it grows taller than any building, greater than a mountain. You can see it's eating the world, and no matter what, it is coming for you. Rushing toward you. And by the time it's blinding, you are terrified and humbled. Watching it, you know it's the kind of thing you should only get to see once. Something that happens once and then never again. We've all seen it so many times, but I still cry, because, when it comes, I know for sure we are infinite. All you feel is infinite, knowing all the falls and leaps and sweet and death that's ever been will be trumped by the wall of nuclear flying at you. You of all people. Then, before you're gone, you know that all that's ever been will still be, even if there are no tomorrows. Even the apocalypse isn't the end. That, you could only know when you're standing before a light so bright it obliterates you. And if you are alone, posed like a dancer, when it comes, you feel silly and scared. And if you are with your family, or anyone at all, when it comes, you feel silly and scared, but at least not alone.

ACKNOWLEDGMENTS AND LOVE

To some incredible instructors, professors, and waymakers: Mrs. Jacobs, Ms. Doctor, Mr. Norton, Sharon Stephenson, Bruce Smith, Brooks Haxton, Chris Kennedy, Mary Karr, Jonathan Dee, Edward Schwarzschild, for seeing what I was and what I could be and bridging the gap.

To James Walley, Tom Frobisher, Anna Mazhirov, Laurie Hobart, Michael Keen, Walker Rutter-Bowman, Jacob Collins-Wilson, Erin Mullikin, Cate McLaughlin, Herve Comeau, Flose Boursiquot, Emilio Sola, and the many writers in my life for giving me something to aspire to.

To Ramapo High School and the East Ramapo Central School District for giving me my fire. To the State University of New York at Albany for the direction. To Terri Zollo and the Cuse Mob for the community and love. To Colgate University for their incredible generosity. To Spring Valley, Rockland County, New York, for giving me a reason.

To Lynne Tillman for the mark-ups, tea, and stories that made this possible.

To Dana Spiotta for her nurturing thoughts and words.

To Arthur Flowers for showing me where the magic is.

To George Saunders for showing me how to laugh in the dark.

To Gerard "Danny" Santiago and the whole Rensselaer connection for first showing me the art of a good story. To the whole Santiago family for the dinners and support. To Kevin Luong for the confidence. To John Smith and Kessly Midy for the laughs. To Kathleen Cancio for being my spirit guide. To Ngan Quan for the unwavering support. To Kapri Rosario and Nini Cancio for necessary happy hours. To Amber Stacks for helping me grow.

To the Fam: Junior Senat, Ashlei Allen, Carl Joseph Louis, Micole Weathers, Nick Creegan, Chidibere Ezemma, Nina Pham, Brittany Williams, Erin Elizabeth, Rob Michael Mathieu, Dance-Nina and Zye Jenkins for all the memories. Love y'all. To the Schwang Gang: Michael Mitchell, Stefan Wells, and Raheem Gumbs for the energy.

To Mark Robinson for your incredible art. To David Hough for your precise eye.

To my truly incredible agent, Meredith Kaffel Simonoff, who believed in this book and made sure it got into the world. I am forever grateful to you.

To my editor, Naomi Gibbs, whose work has brought this book to its highest level. Whose confidence in these stories has been the greatest gift in the world. Again, I am truly grateful to you and all of Houghton Mifflin Harcourt for making this manuscript a book.

To my sisters, Adoma Adjei-Brenyah and Afua Adjei-Brenyah, who showed me what it means to be your uncompromised self.

To my father, who said, "If you have an A+ mind and get a B+, even God will be angry."

To my mother for all the things you said.

"Things My Mother Said" was first published in slightly different form in *Foliate Oak Literary Magazine*, September 2014

"In Retail" was published in *Compose: A Journal of Simply Good Writing*, Fall 2014

"The Finkelstein 5" was published in slightly different form in *Printers Row*, July 2016